DANGER SIGNAL

Chemel's jaw tightened. The tangle of branches concealing the entrance to the observation post bore the clear marks of saw and axe blade—and the Shree could not possibly have advanced to the stage of smelting and metalwork.

She searched behind the branches for what she suspected must be there. Near the entrance, she found it—a thin disk buried in the dirt, obviously a signaling device. Whoever was intervening on Nira must by now know of the team's presence!

She had better get back inside and send off an urgent message to DSC. "Riga," she called as she trotted through the station, "can you—"

She stopped short in the doorway. The team members lay slumped and silent in the control room. There was an unusual odor in the room, like sour citrus. A wave of weakness and cold fear washed through her. She knew that smell—ilyein gas! Then her arms went nerveless and she collapsed full length on the floor.

The Monitor, The Miners and The Shree

LEE KILLOUGH

A Del Rey Book

BALLANTINE BOOKS • NEW YORK

A Del Rey Book
Published by Ballantine Books

Library of Congress Catalog Card Number: 79-91671

ISBN 0-345-28456-9

Manufactured in the United States of America

First Edition: April 1980

Cover art by Wayne Barlowe

To Pat, Friend:
Thanks for all
the help

Chapter One

They made planetfall in darkness. Under contragrav power and with no exterior lights to betray its presence to possible watchers below, the shuttle became a phantom, a black shadow settling silently through the black of Nira's moonless night. The sun's companion star, a brilliant red jewel on the planet's western horizon, was too far away to show a disc or contribute appreciable light.

Inside the shuttle, dark, too, except for the glow of the luminous dials on the control panel, the passengers were also shadows, though not phantoms. From her seat behind the pilot, Chemel Krar listened to the clash and counterpoint of multiple conversations delivered in eight different accents: lisping, clipped, hissing, booming, languid.

"I don't see lights. They're still living with the sun, then."

"I developed it myself. It's a variation on the standard spy eye."

". . . five-hundred-year intervals aren't very long on

an evolutionary scale. How much difference can you expect . . ."

". . . marvelous. When do you unpack one?"

They sounded, Chemel thought, as if they were at a party, not trying to sneak onto a planet for clandestine observations. Perhaps her colleagues considered it a party, or a reunion. Most of them knew each other from previous projects, or had at least read one another's publications.

"It's precisely these small increments of change we are most interested in observing."

"Can I record through it?"

". . . study intelligence from its genesis."

In their excitement, had they considered the problems of the study? Chemel wondered. Had they thought about the factors that might overwhelm them, even force them to scrap the project? Probably not. Studying the Shree was their job. Worrying was hers.

She stared out the port at the planet. Below them lay blackness, featureless as a hole. Problem one: finding the mountain where the station was located in a chain of thousands of peaks, on an isthmus some eighteen-hundred-thousand kord wide.

She rubbed a brow tuft with a long forefinger and frowned at the control panel. She could see the altimeter just beyond the feather-crested silhouette of the pilot. It was winding down very fast.

"We ought to activate the homing signal."

The pilot's crest twitched. "Do we have to? I thought I'd try finding the station by dead reckoning first."

Chemel recognized the sly poke at her in time to bite back the indignant exclamation rising in her throat. Instead, she drew a slow breath. Why did they all find it so amusing that she was serious about her responsibilities as monitor here for the Sodality's Department of Surveys and Charters?

She made her voice bland. "DSC would certainly appreciate our stumbling around over the natives calling attention to ourselves. Activate the signal, if you please."

The pilot shrugged and leaned forward to press a key on the control panel.

Chemel watched the gridded screen above the key. She rubbed her brow tuft. That signal had been set as the last study team left. Almost anything could have happened to it in the intervening five hundred years. If it did not activate, they would have to try dead reckoning, and that would not be easy at night. A daylight search was out of the question; they would almost certainly be seen.

For several long minutes the screen remained black. Behind Chemel, the chatter continued unabated and unconcerned. Finally, a light bloomed in the upper left quadrant of the screen. Chemel let out her breath. The homer was alive.

The pilot maneuvered the shuttle until the light lay in the middle of the screen. He took them in along the signal, following it like a diver going down an achor chain. The companion sun disappeared behind Nira.

Chemel peered out the port, wishing she could see something of the surface. She had seen the tapes made by previous teams, of course. The station lay in beautiful country, which miners fifteen hundred years ago had christened the Treasure Mountains. The steep, rugged chain rose spectacularly high, as was possible on light-gravity worlds, and cradled verdant green valleys between them. What had impressed her most during the briefings were the cliffs. The thought of those towering rock faces made Chemel itch to feel them under her hands and climbing boots.

She shook herself. This train of thought was fruitless, a waste of energy. There would be no climbing on Nira.

The shuttle shuddered. Chemel frowned. Wind already? She glanced at the altimeter again. Yes, wind already. The atmosphere, too, reached much higher and thinned more slowly than on worlds with heavier gravity.

The homing light swung to one side of the screen, then the other as the shuttle bucked through a rough layer of air. Presently the air steadied and the shuttle stopped bucking. The homing light centered again.

"Ground in five minutes," the pilot called out.

Chemel cleared her throat. "Your attention, team."

Conversation died. Chemel swung toward them, even though she could not see them. She smelled their warm mixture of alien scents and listened to the sigh of their collective breathing. "We're near ground. As you know, sound can carry through the hull, so perhaps we ought to remain quiet for the rest of the descent. I'll leave the ship first and locate the station entrance. Wear your infrared goggles. Don't use hand lamps. We don't want to risk—"

"Detection by the natives." Jiahano Kamisanuaga's voice crowded in, his long vowels and soft, slurred consonants gently shouldering her words aside. "We know, *mua.*"

Chemel felt a flush heat her face. *Mua* was a Mianai word for child. She knew she should not take the remark personally—Jiahano was a hundred and fifty years old, after all. Most members of other races were children to him. Still, it was a reminder that of the team, only Prol Dottar, one of the surveillance electronics technologists, was younger than she.

"We'll unload the shuttle as quickly as possible after the station is opened," Chemel continued. "The supply shuttle can start down as soon as this one lifts off. I estimate the local time near midnight. That gives us a little less than five hours before dawn, and we will need to have everything in the station by then."

As the spinning needle of the altimeter slowed, Chemel peered out the port again and could now see some detail. Even without moonlight, the snow topping the peaks had a visibly higher albedo, like islands in a black sea. Then as the shuttle sank below the altitude of the taller peaks, irregular patches of stars disappeared, blotted out by the mountains.

The shuttle trembled through another stream of air, then steadied again. Moments later the sense of motion stopped, and Chemel glanced at the altimeter. It had stopped moving. As she watched, the needle wavered and dropped a fraction more, to zero. The shuttle jarred once then was still.

Flipping off the switches, the pilot announced: "Ground." Then he swiveled around and released his safety belt.

Chemel pulled on her goggles. Through them, she watched him cross the shuttle and undog the hatch. Releasing her own safety belt, she picked up her pack and groped in it for the station key, an instrument resembling, in size and design, a hand computer.

The pilot opened the hatch. As it slid aside, a wave of chilly air rushed in at them. Chemel slung her pack on her shoulder, crossed to the opening, and stepped out onto a ramp. Three strides later, she stood on Nira's soil. After the stuffy heat of the shuttle, she welcomed the stinging cold on her face and hands, and the fiery burn of it in her nose with each breath she took. The temperature was pleasant, like that of a mild summer night at home. She exhaled and watched the steaming cloud of her breath swirl around her before dissipating into the night air.

The night smelled intriguingly alien—of snow and of something sweetly organic. The air also carried the sound of rain, though no moisture touched her skin. After a minute she decided the sound came from the grove of trees upslope, from leaves rattling together in the wind. Overhead, strange star patterns glittered brilliantly through the clear air.

Chemel pushed forward, taking an experimental step. The effort took her farther than she intended. She stumbled but caught herself before she fell. A second step was better balanced. The transport ship and the shuttle had been maintained at point eight five of standard gravity, as many space vessels with mixed crews were. Nira's pull was a point lighter yet.

Once she was sure of her footing, Chemel looked around. Through the goggles, she saw the outline of the terrain. The shuttle rested on a relatively level bench meadow on an otherwise steep mountainside. Trees grew in thick groves upslope and down. Upslope and to her left, the ground broke, exposing a rough rock face about two kord high at its widest part. The rocks ran some ten to twelve kord in each direction before narrowing and allowing the upper and lower levels of the ground to rejoin one another.

Her fingers tightened on the key. DSC records showed the station entrance in a rock face. Could this be it, still intact, unchanged after five hundred years? She would have expected more ground shift on a planet with the vigorous tectonic activity of this one. She pointed the key at the rock face and tapped the activator button.

The indicator light on the face of the key flickered dimly. She pushed her goggles up on her forehead so she could see the light's color. It glowed yellow. The key point was near, then, but she would have to hunt for it. Slowly, Chemel swung the key, scanning the rock face. The light intensified, turning orange, then red. As the flicker stopped, Chemel moved forward, holding the key steady, watching the red deepen toward purple. She knew she was pointed at the entrance now. The lock point should be close.

Then, without any warning, something cracked her across the shins. This time she did fall, pitching headlong into branches that jabbed her and caught her jacket and scratched her face and hands. She did not realize she had yelled until she heard running footsteps and felt strong hands on her arms helping her back up onto her feet.

"Shhh," Prol Dottar whispered. "We don't want the Shree to hear us."

"Are you all right?" The sibilant accent, dry as sand, belonged to the Cheolon anthropologist Zeema Sheth.

"I'm fine." She pulled her goggles down to see what had tripped her.

It was a windfall. The twisted tangle of brush and trees lay clumped along the end of the rock face—right in front of what the key indicated should be the station entrance. Chemel swore. They would need hours to move the branches. Worse, though, was the fact that doing so would leave obvious evidence of their presence and activity.

She retrieved the key from where she had dropped it in the brush and considered what to do. As she circled the windfall, Chemel held the key aimed so the light remained bright violet. Perhaps they could make use of the brush. It certainly helped to conceal the entrance. Suppose they removed only part of it—

The thought broke off. She stared. Behind the windfall a narrow space lay between brush and rock. What luck. Hardly able to believe it, she reached out to feel the gap. Her hands confirmed what her eyes saw. She estimated the gap to be about the width of her shoulders, perhaps a bit narrower. By turning sideways, she would have no trouble at all sliding through it.

Dropping her pack by the windfall, she then edged in along the rock face, keeping the key in front of her. While she watched the signal light, she also remained alert for signs of any wildlife that might be using the space as a den. She saw no animals.

Suddenly the key's light flared. Chemel peered at it from under her goggles. The light was now bright blue. She was very close to the lock on the entrance! Quickly, she tapped out the lock combination on the numbered buttons of the key's face.

She heard no sound, but felt something like a sharp point being pulled quickly through her brain. Metal scraped rock. Chemel could see nothing, with or without her goggles. Deactivating the key, she shoved it into a thigh pocket of her jumpsuit, and began exploring the rock face with her hands. Her fingers touched a crack, and she followed it. The crack ran vertically up the rock face, then near the top it turned to run horizontally. Shortly thereafter it turned downward. This has to be it, she decided. Pressing both hands flat against the rock, Chemel pushed. A section of rock swung in.

Chemel slid a cautious foot forward into the hole it left. When her foot found an edge, she was glad she had been cautious. The level inside lay a healthy step below the ground outside. Had it been built that way or had the ground outside risen that far in five hundred years?

She slipped her hand lamp off her belt and tapped it on, playing the red beam around her. She was standing in a chamber about a kord wide and three deep. The staleness of the air in it choked her. A second door closed off the far end of the chamber. She pulled out the key and punched a second combination. The sharp point scraped her brain again and the inner door loosened. A push would open it, too, but she did not go any farther for the time being. The air inside would surely be deader than that in the entry lock.

Before anyone could move in, they would have to pump fresh air into the station. Time to bring in the technical crew.

She slid back out along the rock face into the open and groped in her pack for the station manual. "Prol, will you bring Riga and Akaara here?"

Prol returned minutes later accompanied by Riga Lodao, their other elec-tech, and Akaara Osthoo, the computer technologist. Chemel led all three to the entry lock, where she pulled out the station manual and handed it to them. "How do we get air in there to breathe?"

The three of them put their heads together over the manual.

"We can open the vents," Riga said. Chemel knew from her dossier that Riga was over fifty standard years, with a married daughter and grandchildren back on her native world Lazo. "We'll have to start up the generator for a thorough air exchange, though."

Chemel had studied the manual during the trip out from Center. "The generator is in the first room to the right inside."

And it was five hundred years old . . . five hundred years of being inactive. They had a replacement unit coming on the supply shuttle, as they had parts to upgrade all the equipment, but until the replacements were installed, they had to live with the antiques.

She pulled an oxygen mask from her pack and slipped it over her mouth and nose. "Let's see what it looks like, shall we?"

The scene appeared nightmarish as they filed into the station. The empty corridor did not echo as she expected. Instead, it absorbed every sound, so that their voices, already muffled by the masks, died around them. Their feet made almost no sound at all, and as they moved, the red beams from their hand lamps cast distorted shadows on the walls.

Fortunately they found the generator without difficulty and stood for a few minutes, playing their beams over it. Prol hissed something through his teeth in his own language.

Chemel echoed him with a profanity of her own. Though no expert on machinery like this, she still knew this generator could not be a mere five hundred years old. It had probably been installed during the first update study a millennium ago. Filmed with a light powdering of dust, it loomed like some prehistoric beast. Then, distracted for a moment, Chemel noticed the remarkably small amount of dust in the station and was impressed. The seals had held tight. "See what you can do with it."

"Affirm," Akaara responded cheerfully.

Chemel left to organize the unloading of the shuttle, and found it already well underway. Such baggage as they had brought with them was being piled in a neat stack beside the windfall, waiting for the signal to move it into the station.

Chemel nodded in satisfaction. With the unloading under control, she had time to consider the problem of moving people into the station. Most of the team would have no difficulty going through the passage. Even Kiris Di-ra-Ithai should be able to navigate it, if she kept her wings folded tight. Baezar Pezetaku was the problem. The Azcarn not only had broad shoulders, both sets, but being four-footed made him wider front to back than side to side. Could he fit through?

She found him and explained the situation. "Later we can cut the windfall back a bit from the inside, but this first time you'll have to get through however you can."

"It isn't as if I plan daily trips outside." The anthropologist's booming voice sounded more amused than concerned. "Just two passages are absolutely necessary, tonight's and when we leave. Somehow I'll make myself fit. Sheth, would you hold this?"

He unsnapped the blanketlike garment he wore and handed it to Zeema Sheth.

The passage was tight. Chemel, following the Azcarn, heard him grunt a number of times and even gasp once or twice. When he finally reached the entry lock and she was able to check him over with her hand lamp, her tongue ticked against her teeth in surprise. No wonder he had gasped. He was missing a large piece of hide from his upper left shoulder and left hip, no doubt scraped off on the rocks. His right side had been gouged liberally by sharp ends of branches in the windfall, and his broad, flat face was twisted in a wry grimace that robbed it of its usual dignity. "I believe I'll wait for you to cut back the brush before I leave. I'm not masochist enough to enjoy being flayed."

At that moment, Riga leaned out through the inner door. "We're having trouble with the light circuits, but at least the ventilation is operational now."

Chemel passed the word to the team members still

outside, then went to check through the rest of the station, which resembled nothing so much as the transport they had just left in orbit. The rooms and passages cut into the mountain rock were sealed and paneled with the same metal and plastic found in most spacegoing vessels. The major difference was that instead of sporting bland colors, the panels had been decorated with murals. A planetscape from a different Sodality world decorated every room. Some even filled an entire wall, giving a viewer the impression of looking out through a window. Others that circled the entire room were so graphic that Chemel felt the sucking dryness of the Cheolon desert and the humid chill of the Aranen highlands more vividly than she smelled the mustiness of dust and stale air actually around her.

The furniture, stripped to its frames, without cushions or mattresses, was ready for those things to arrive on the supply shuttle.

Though the station had appeared large on the manual map, it seemed to be even larger as she toured it by the light of her hand lamp. She discovered rooms designed for every purpose: commons, galley, sleeping, workshops, recreation, even a library. The hangar stood empty. But as soon as the transport unloaded them, it would hold a sky scooter and an air sled. She even found a greenhouse that almost looked like an outside garden and an observation room where shutters, carefully camouflaged from the outside, could be opened to look out on Nira itself.

It seemed an extravagant amount of space for their party of nine people, but she understood the reason for it. They were going to be shut in here together for five years. Though every member of the team had been chosen for his scientific expertise and a high compatibility index, without some way to escape from one another occasionally, the study could end in productiveless bickering, enmity, and even mass murder.

Chemel sniffed. The air smelled noticeably fresher. She filled her lungs with its sweetness as she stood peering out through the shutters. Not that there was much to see except the star fields overhead and the pale blurs of snow-topped peaks facing the observation window. Dawn was still almost three hours away. As much as she wanted to see Nira, she wished the planet did not have such a short rotation period. The team could use a longer night.

In her line of sight, a star disappeared; then one next to it did likewise. A moment later, the first reappeared, followed by the second. Chemel noted the phenomenon with considerable interest. Something was flying out there. More stars blinked out and reappeared. A night bird? Perhaps one of the natives? They had not been nocturnal before, but as sentient beings they would not have to be limited to "normal" activity periods. Whatever it was, was flying in a line that took it in front of the opposite peaks. She strained, trying to make out the shape of the flyer.

Little more was visible than a dark blur moving across a pale one, but the sight made her frown. That was no animal. The shape was too sqaure, like an aircraft. Had the pilot lifted off without waiting for her okay? Chemel slapped the shutters closed and headed for the communications room. She was going to burn his ears off, right up to his feather crest.

Suddenly the lights blinked on. Chemel stopped short, squeezing her eyes closed against the pain of the glare. In the air above her head, she heard Riga's voice. "We now have a fully operational generator."

And a working intercom, too, it appeared. Chemel wished Riga had used it to give warning before blinding them with the lights.

Someone near Chemel cheered. She eased her eyes open.

She stood in the commons room. Around her, the members of the study team were squinting at one another. After hours of considering them only as individual sounds and scents, seeing them in the light struck Chemel with their specie variety. Three were saurian:

Jiahano of the pastel-blue hide and liquid-smooth lines; Sheth, mustard yellow, lizardlike in his angularity; and Akaara, ebony black with muscles sliding powerfully under his sleek hide. Kiris was avian. The rest came in assorted mammalian types, bipedal except for the hexapodal Baezar.

"How soon can we activate the computer?" Salah Kufarol asked. "I'd like to start feeding the known Shree vocabulary into the memory."

The linguist no doubt intended the question for the technical people, but Chemel chose to answer. "If we need the computer for basic station operation, we'll activate it. Otherwise, we'll wait until all the equipment and supplies have been moved in."

She was careful to keep her voice neutral. Chemel had still not decided how she felt about Salah. On the one hand, they were racial sisters. There was even a physical resemblance—the same tall build and pale coloring, the same ash-white hair and yellow eyes. However, Salah's ancestors had left Virini to colonize Liakandra six thousand years ago because they practiced beliefs the Virinians of the time found unacceptably radical. As if reflecting the philosophical difference that still separated their worlds, Salah was soft and plump where Chemel was proudly lean and bony.

"I don't want to activate the computer," Akaara put in, "until the new modules have been added." He looked around. "Does anyone have anything left on the shuttle or can we send it up and bring the supply shuttle down?"

Chemel started. *The shuttle*. She had been on her way to the communications room to— The meaning of Akaara's comment suddenly registered. She frowned. "What? You mean the shuttle hasn't left yet?"

"No. Why?"

"But, I saw—" She broke off.

They looked at her.

"Is everything off the shuttle?" she asked.

They indicated yes in their varied gestures.

"Then I'll tell the pilot to lift off." She walked outside, where the shuttle still sat on the bench. Giving the pilot orders to lift, she stood back, watching the craft through her goggles as it rose skyward. She ran a hand through the short thatch of her hair, puzzled. She had seen an aircraft from the observation room. She was sure of that. Obviously what she saw could not have been the shuttle. Surely the natives were too primitive to build aircraft, even if they wanted to. So . . . what was the aircraft? And, more important, whose was it?

Chapter Two

The dawn hawk wheeled around the commons room in full flight, gray and white wings flashing. It climbed toward the ceiling, then without warning, dived straight for Salah, its talons spread. The linguist laughed, but nonetheless ducked, covering her head with her arms.

"Prol!" Chemel snapped. "Salah, we're supposed to be—"

They never heard her. Prol's fingers played over the control box in his hand and the hawk soared again.

"He's absolutely beautiful, Prol," Riga said. "When I was directing security for my family's winery I experimented with training birds to fly rounds carrying spy eyes, but I never considered anything as complex as building my own bird. Congratulations."

Prol's smoky eyes lighted. "The cameras are located in its eyes and each sees an entire hundred-and-eighty-degree arc. The transmitter in its head will send everything back to our screens here. It has IR capability, too, for night flights." He brought the mechanical hawk down toward the floor, made it hover, then set it down in a perfect four-legged landing.

"Team," Chemel called.

"What about sound transmission?" Salah asked.

"There's that, too."

Chemel flung herself back in her chair. As a conference, this meeting was a failure. Was she the only one who cared about procedure? What possessed them? How did they find the energy to carry on like this? They had been driving themselves like robots, working almost around the clock for the past five days, upgrading or replacing equipment, making the station livable. They should be exhausted. Instead, they were all playing games with Prol's surveillance devices. All except Jiahano, of course, who sat to one side with a faint, aloof smile.

He turned to meet her eyes. "They are celebrating the conclusion of housekeeping and the commencement of our real work."

Chemel stiffened. Was he a telepath? Mianai were not reported to be, but they revealed so little of themselves to other races, who could say?

"It is not telepathy," Jiahano said. "When one has accumulated a certain amount of experience with people one begins to make deductions based on observed reactions and behavior."

That remark did nothing to reassure her he was not reading her mind, but she did not choose to challenge him. If he were a telepath, he knew how she felt. If he were not, there was no point in making herself seem paranoid. "Housekeeping isn't over yet. That's what this conference is supposed to be about. We still have two observation posts to open, you know."

Jiahano considered. After a minute he wrinkled his scalp, where a fine layer of dark-blue scales gave him the look of wearing a lace cap. "The transport is gone, is it not?"

"Yes. It left orbit a couple of hours ago."

"Then opening those posts cannot be critical or it would have remained until they were operational."

"Not critical doesn't mean not important!"

He wrinkled his scalp again. "However, it does mean we can delay the task without harm. Be patient, *mua*. There is a universe of time and all things may be accomplished, each in its turn."

Chemel looked away from him, sighing. She watched Kiris circle the mech. The anthropologist wrapped the toes of one foot around it. Lifting it to where she could grasp it with the thumb and free digit on each of her wings, Kiris stretched the mech out in front of her. "I hate your toy, Prol." The relative immobility of her beak, as compared to lips, gave her a pronounced lisp. "It's unfair to let a mere machine fly anywhere while I'm forced to sit caged."

Chemel grimaced. Kiris was not the only one who longed to go out. Every time Chemel saw the facing cliffs from the observation room, her blood raced. There had been cliffs like that above their cabin in the Kadrol Highlands where her family had spent most holidays. Chemel had climbed them countless times after she was first dragged bodily up them by her mother and brother at the age of six.

Why she longed to climb now, she did not understand. Athe Krar had insisted, over the weak protests of Chemel's father, on teaching her children all her favorite sports. Klen threw himself into them with the same mad glitter in his eyes their mother had, but for Chemel it had always been a mixture of excitement and terror. Sometimes she froze on the rock face, gluing her body to the cliff while the wind whipped at her, bringing the smells of mountain trees and the chill of the snow still decorating the peak above them. Risking her life this way was insane, something in her whispered, and she would not be able to move.

"Come on," Athe Krar would yell up from below. "Prove you're my daughter and not like that piece of furniture who carried you for me."

That taunt never failed to move Chemel to prove she was all Krar and had not absorbed anything of her broodmother through the placenta during gestation. What fearful times those climbs were, though. When she finally reached solid ground, sweating and trembling, she always swore she would never go up again, and yet here she was, aching for it. Madness. She shook her head.

"My wings will atrophy to nothing," Kiris said.

Chemel's mouth tightened. "You knew the conditions when you joined the study team. You know why the conditions exist, too."

Kiris blinked at the whipcrack in Chemel's voice. "I know," she said. Her tone was low, placating. "I agree with the noninterference policy. I'm just so envious of that machine." She paused. "I can miss flying, can't I?"

"It's all right," Prol said. "We'll sneak you out at night for a turn around the mountain."

Chemel came up out of her chair. "You will not! If we reveal ourselves to these people, even if we intervene in the slightest respect, DSC will pull us back to Center so fast we'll arrive the day before we left."

Prol frowned. "Maybe Kiris understands DSC's policy, but I don't. On the transport Salah and Jiahano talked about studying the Woon and digging out their cities. The Woon aren't a spacing race and never have been, but we come and go from Piloo all the time and no one has ever screamed that we're interfering with the Woon's evolution."

"The Woon are *devolving*," Salah said. "It's morally proper to stop a decline and help them start back toward realizing their potential."

"I don't dispute your Lseumist beliefs," Sheth said, "but I think the reason we have free access to Piloo is that the Virinians established contact with them during the building of their empire and everyone has automatically included it in each succeeding interworld organization in this sector."

"Whatever the policy toward the Woon, the one in

force here is strict nonintervention." Chemel looked straight at Prol. "No one is to leave the station at any time except when taking the scooter or sled to one of the observation posts."

Prol stared back. "This is a nice job for you, isn't it? The Virinian Coalition may be gone but you can still make people do what you think is best for them."

That was too much! DSC must have incorrectly measured his compatibility index. Chemel started for him, a hand clenching . . . only to bump her belt buckle into Baezar's shoulder on the first step.

He smiled up at her in apology. "Sorry. Did I blunder in your way?"

The seconds he needed to speak gave her time to regain control. She unclenched her hand. "I don't think you blundered." She sat down again.

In the strained silence that followed, Kiris said, "I'll learn to like watching Prol's bird fly. And I guess I'll take up isometrics."

"Would you like to fly it yourself?" Prol picked up the mech and held it out to her. "It needs a test outside."

Kiris blinked at him. "That's sweet, but I'd better not. I'm an anthrolopologist, not an elec-tech. I'd probably wreck it."

The tension eased. Prol shrugged. "It still needs a test flight. Anyone want to send it somewhere in particular?"

The observation posts were too far away, but there was one site nearby Chemel considered of passing interest. "We're just up the mountain from Megeyn's old camp. Let's see what it looks like now."

Prol frowned quizzically. "Megeyn's old camp?"

"Don't you know Niran history?" Salah asked.

"I never looked it up. Why should I? It doesn't affect my job."

"I never thought to look it up, either," Riga said. "All I know is we've been making studies of these people every five hundred years. Now you've made me ashamed of my ignorance. Who was Megeyn?"

Chemel opened her mouth to answer but Akaara started first. "Megeyn was a Thajan mining company. Fifteen hundred years ago they had a charter for mining Nira."

"With a sentient species here?" Prol asked.

"No one thought there was one then. The charter inspection said the planet was uninhabited by anything even close to being sentient. Twelve years after the charter was granted, though, a doctor working for Megeyn filed a sentient species claim. An investigation was made and the Shree were ruled sentient, whereupon Megeyn was kicked off the planet and the study teams moved in."

Prol frowned. "Twelve years? That's impossible. No species could go from animal to human in just twelve years."

"The doctor proved the Shree were attacking and killing miners using daggerthorn branches poisoned with sweetvine juice. That's certainly a mark of intelligence."

"But . . . *twelve years?*"

"The theory was the Shree were protosentient," Sheth explained. "They had the brain capacity for rational thought; they just weren't using it . . . until competition from the miners made them use it. According to the studies, most of the Shree are still essentially animal. The intelligent bands occupy an area stretching about seven-hundred-thousand kord in each direction from here."

Baezar nodded. "I'm hoping we'll find they're starting to spread out across the planet now. Well, shall we see what remains of the mining camp after fifteen hundred years?"

Prol headed for the station entrance with his mech.

They would have to arrange something so that they would not have to open the entrance for the spy-eye devices, Chemel thought, but for now she let Prol go with only a warning. "Don't step outside until you're sure the area is clear."

Prol was back shortly without the mech. He led the way to the communications and computer room. "We'll control and watch its progress from here. The hand control is good for no more than a few hundred kord."

A bank of screens stretched above the control panel. Similview headsets lay on a shelf beside it. As Prol's hands played over the controls, an image of the scene outside the station entrance came up on the screens.

Chemel plugged one of the headsets into the panel and slid it down over her eyes and ears. At once she seemed to be outside. The illusion was not perfect; it was a scentless, nontactile world, but through the mech's "eyes" and "ears" she could at least see and hear everything it could "see" and "hear."

How strange it felt to be observing the rock face and windfall from ground level. They looked different by daylight, too. Now she realized why Baezar had lost hide. The surface of the rock, moving past her in small jerks as the mech walked toward open ground, cast pointed shadows on itself, and the ends of the brush protruded in wicked points.

Something about that brush bothered her. She started to turn for a closer look, but had forgotten she was just a passenger. The mech's strides continued unchecked. In another moment it was on open ground. Then it sprang into the air.

"Where's this mining camp?" Prol's voice asked through the rush of wind in Chemel's ears.

"Straight down the mountain."

Prol did not send the mech there immediately. First it climbed, and the mountain seemed to fall away. Chemel blinked in the glaring light of Nira's white sun. After a moment, though, the light intensity dropped.

"Notice the photo-response of the lenses," Prol said.

"Beautiful," Riga exclaimed.

Chemel found her point of reference personalizing. It was not the mech flying; she was. She climbed higher, up through a cloud layer, and quickly forgot all about the brush and gave herself up to her eyes and ears. She wheeled and dipped in the white sunlight, soaring through the azure sky, cutting clouds with her wings.

"It looks nice, but the experience isn't the same." Kiris sighed. "Unless you can feel the push of the air on your wings and the rush of cold past your feathers, it's just a picture."

"Picky, picky." Under the light tone in Prol's voice lay disappointment.

"I'm impressed," Sheth said. "Do you have any other mechs, something we could use to move right in among the Shree?"

"I have a burrow cat. I'm told the Shree keep them in their caves to clean up the vermin."

"Good. But how do we get it to a Shree cave? Can the hawk carry it?" Baezar asked.

"It's too heavy for the hawk. I'll send it out by remote contragrav carrier during the night."

Chemel wished they would all stop chattering. She wanted to enjoy the flight. "I thought you were going to take the mech to the mining camp."

There was a pause. "Of course," Prol said. "Hold on to your feathers."

Suddenly Chemel felt as if she was plummeting down through the clouds and sky like a stone, and she fought to keep in mind that this was just a broadcast, not her falling. Still, she wanted to spread arms and legs across the air and create some wind resistance, to slow the dive. She wanted to reach for contragrav harness controls. Instead, she was a helpless passenger and the mountainside rushed up at her unchecked.

"I don't see any sign of a camp," Prol called.

"The buildings were all removed when Megeyn left," Akaara said. "I guess nature has wiped out the rest."

The mech's descent had not slowed.

"Do you plan to smash the spy eye?" Chemel asked. She was surprised at the calm in her voice, as her nails dug into the palms of her hands. The world spun under her, the horizon flinging itself crazily down and sideways. Her stomach lurched. She closed her eyes.

"Prol, please." The protest was voiced simultaneously from several people.

Through their voices came Jiahano's, languid as always. "Look a hundred twenty degrees up to the left."

Chemel opened her eyes again. Above the mech, dark against the sky, flew another winged form.

Soft sighs from seven throats reached her through the sound of wind in her ears. Here was their first Shree. They had seen tapes of Shree in briefings, of course, so they knew what the species looked like. But seeing one in the flesh was different. No matter that the eyes they saw it with were those of a camera.

Prol sent the mech up toward the Shree.

"Not too close," Kiris said. "A real dawn hawk would keep a safe distance."

The Shree peered down at the mech. Its amber eyes were brightly curious in its flat face. Its large ears, belling out from the sides of its head, pricked forward.

The being was small, with a copper-brown coat of thick velvety fur. Chemel estimated that standing, the creature's head would reach a little above the middle of her chest. Slender limbs suggested it was lightweight, too, though the powerful flight muscles of its chest and back gave it a stocky look about the shoulders, especially the upper shoulders where its wings grew. Arms were attached to a second shoulder girdle lower on its thorax. The hands had three fingers and an opposable thumb.

Dark, thin membrane made up the wings, stretching between its wing finger bones and attached to its body from shoulder to hip, then to its tail and heels, but leaving its legs free. It had used that fact in designing the equipment harness it wore. The harness, with its pouches and loops, ran around the Shree's neck and down the front of its trunk before looping behind its thighs.

"Prol," Kiris pleaded. "Back off."

Chemel felt too close to the Shree, too. Its eyes were regarding the "hawk" with uncomfortably intense interest.

"Keep below it," Kiris said. "She has to keep her wings taut to maintain lift, so she can't fold them to dive."

"Perhaps we should withdraw altogether. No genuine dawn hawk would be aloft at midday."

Jiahano might be right. Chemel was about to second him when the Shree somersaulted downward with blinding speed, wings sweeping forward together. Kiris shrieked, but Prol could not move the mech in time. Caught in the created turbulence, it was pulled toward the Shree, who caught it easily in its hands.

Prol swore. Chemel pulled off her headset and found the elec-tech working frantically with his controls. On the screen above the panel, reaching talons and flailing wings made peripheral blurs as the mech struggled. The Shree held fast, hissing through its nose with a sound like laughter.

"Do you have any defensive circuits in that thing?" she asked. "Electric shock?"

"The next one will have." Prol's tone was grim.

On the screen, the view of the Shree's head became obscured by a hand coming toward the mech's head. Was the Shree going to wring the "hawk's" neck?

If so, the Shree changed its mind. The hand paused, and beyond it the Shree cocked its head and held the mech out at arms' length.

Prol continued to play over his controls. The mech thrashed, but its wings were pinned and it could not reach the Shree's arms with either talons or beak. The beat of the Shree's wings never paused. Prol swore long and passionately.

"I don't suppose you have a self-destruct device in the mech, either," Chemel said.

Prol bent his head over the controls without answering.

Chemel sighed.

Salah leaned toward the screen, head to one side. "Listen. He's singing. They have music."

Chemel had not paid much attention to the sounds the Shree was making. She listened now. Yes, there was definitely a musical pattern to the sounds, repetitious, though, as in a chant. The words, murmured almost under the Shree's breath, contained more music than the "melody." The syllables mixed clicks and whistles, similar to the K'keewhee language. Perhaps they should have brought along a K'keewhee linguist instead of Salah. They could easily have turned one of the station's sleeping rooms into an aquarium to accommodate the aquatic mammal.

"Can you understand any of it?" Baezar asked.

Salah closed her eyes and listened. Presently she opened them again, shaking her head. "My vocabulary is five hundred years out of date. The best I can do is a word here and there." She frowned. "There was one odd word, though." Her frown deepened.

"Yes?" Chemel prompted.

"He used one that sounded just like the Panlingua word for *machine*."

"Coincidence, probably." Chemel knew several cases of words in different languages sounding the same. The Virinian word for *hunter*, for instance, could easily be confused with the Dakisi word for *time*.

"Look," Riga said. "He's taking us home."

Chemel replaced her headset. Most of her vision was dominated by the Shree's chest and harness, but part of the right eye saw an approaching cliff face. The rock was scattered with ledges and cave openings. The Shree backpedaled in the air and landed on its feet on a ledge.

Half a dozen other adult and young Shree lay on their stomachs on the ledge, sunning themselves. They looked up as the Shree landed and called a greeting, or what Chemel presumed to be a greeting. It sounded like an expiration of breath and three clicks. Then to her consternation, the Shree thrust the mech out toward the others.

Chemel swore. "The next one of those leaving here has a self-destruct device in it. Isn't there anything you can do with this one to get it away?"

A chorus of protests greeted her question.

"Leave it."

"Don't do anything, Prol."

Chemel jerked off her headset. "That is a sophisticated alien artifact in the hands of primitive people. It's forbidden."

The four anthropologists and the linguist all wore headsets. They had become totally engrossed in what the mech's eyes were transmitting.

"It's just what we need." Kiris snapped her beak in excitement. "It's brought us right in there with them."

"Record this, Prol," Sheth said.

Chemel ran her hand through her hair. The situation was terrible. How was she going to explain it to her superiors? She should have thought to ask about defense and self-destruct circuits before she ever let Prol send the blasted mech out.

"There it is again," Salah said. "They said the Pan word for *machine*."

Chemel put on the headset again. She wanted to hear what was going on for herself. It was probably just coincidence as she thought before, but it would be prudent to check for certain.

She did not hear the word again, but what she saw first puzzled her, then sent fingers of apprehension trailing down her spine, and finally filled her with thundering waves of horror and indignation.

The Shree bent over the mech, prodding and poking it. One of them flexed the mech's wings. After some discussion, the Shree that brought the mech in pulled a knife from a loop on its body harness. It slit the mech's skin and peeled it back. When it had flayed the mech, the Shree and the others poked into the network of wiring and understructure beneath.

There was something disquieting about seeing "oneself" dissected "alive," but that was not what made Chemel tear off the headset with shaking hands. It was the way the Shree went about the dissection. Their dark and amber eyes held interest and curiosity, and some surprise, but nowhere did Chemel detect any sign of the incomprehension or fear to be expected in primitive people confronted by something beyond their experience.

There could be other explanations, perhaps, but the simplest and most obvious was that the mech was *not* beyond their experience. The Shree had proceeded with such sureness. That knife, too, was a beautiful blade.

She thought of the Shree word that sounded like the Pan *machine*. Then she remembered a square, dark shape against the mountains the night they arrived. She also remembered that something had bothered her about the windfall when the mech left the station.

Chemel tore out of the communications room toward the station entrance. She did not even bother to make sure the area was clear before stepping outside. All that interested her, all she could see, was the ends of the brush.

Discovering what had bothered her when she saw them through the mech's eyes was not difficult. Branches broken off of trees should have splintered ends. On these branch ends, however, the surface was a clean, oblique cut with the marks of saw and axe blade clearly visible in the wood.

Her jaw tightened. The windfall had not occurred naturally. It had been deliberately built there. The previous team could not have been responsible, nor the Shree—her finger traced the sharp edge of an axe cut—not unless they had progressed phenomenally in the past five hundred years to the point of high-quality smelting and smithing. So, the agent responsible was an outsider, a non-Niran. And that together with everything else meant one thing—*intervention*.

DSC had to be told.

Chemel started back into the station, then hesitated, frowning at the windfall. For the first time it occurred to her to wonder why it had been built. Not to block the entrance or the space would not have been left along the rock face.

She rubbed a brow tuft. Perhaps the question was not why build the windfall but why leave space behind it? Whoever was here on Nira must know that their presence was illegal. The windfall indicated they knew about the observation station, and therefore about the Niran study. They would need to know when the study group arrived in order to start covering their tracks. That could explain why she saw the ship the night they arrived; it was patrolling, keeping watch for them. Could that also be the reason for the passage along the rock face?

Breaking off a branch from the windfall, Chemel dropped to her hands and knees. She squeezed along the rock face in a crawl, repeatedly jabbing the branch into the ground ahead of her. It was a tight fit. The rock scraped even through the fabric of her jumpsuit. She did not have to bear it long, though. Less than a kord from the entrance her stick encountered resistance. She wrapped both hands around the stick and used it as a digging tool. In a minute she had uncovered an object lying buried under a thin layer of earth.

The disk was thin, slightly convex in shape, and about a hand's breadth in diameter. It appeared to be made of plastic and flattened when pressure was applied. Chemel did not know the name for it, or exactly how it worked, but she could guess the purpose. When someone came down the passage and stepped on the disk, it sent out a signal—which meant that whoever was on Nira must know by now that the study team was there.

She backed hurriedly toward the entrance. One of the elec-techs could tell her for certain if the disk were what she thought. After that, she had better activate the tachyon communicator and tell DSC what was going on.

"Riga," she called as she trotted through the station toward the communications room. "Riga, can you—"

She stopped short in the doorway, her question dying in her throat. Riga and Prol were both slumped across the control panel. On the floor lay the rest of the team, still wearing headsets.

Chemel dropped to her knees beside Baezar, the closest one, and felt his throat for a pulse. What had happened? Baezar was still alive anyway. The pulse beat strong and steady under her finger.

Then she noticed an unusual odor. She sniffed. It smelled like sour citrus, and vaguely familiar.

A wave of weakness washed through her, accompanied by cold fear. Now she recognized the smell—ilyein gas! She crawled for the door. Outside . . . she had to reach outside. She must not breathe any more of the air in here. Must not . . .

It was the last thought she had before her arms became nerveless, too, and she collapsed full length on the floor.

Chapter Three

She was still conscious, Chemel discovered. Why, she did not know. Ilyein normally rendered everyone who breathed it instantly and totally unconscious, and kept them that way for up to five hours. DSC often used the stuff when agents or monitors needed to examine beings or structures in a nonintervention area without being seen by the local inhabitants. They would spray the area, go in as soon as the air was clear to do what they had to, and get out before everyone woke up. Perhaps the circulation system was already scrubbing out the gas when she came in, so that she received only a diluted amount.

Consciousness was the limit, however. She could not move. All her willpower would not so much as shift her eyes, and it was only from a misty distance that she could hear and see. What she heard sent cold washing down her spine—footsteps.

That ought to be impossible. She had closed the door behind her as she came in, which automatically locked it. No one without a key could open it from the outside.

From where she lay in the doorway of the communications room, she saw mostly floor, but her field of vision also included some of the corridor. Into that area of corridor walked a pair of feet. They were scaled, with long, mobile toes. Feathers grew down the legs to the ankles. A wing tip with its aerie markings of blue-dyed feather tips was also visible. Since Kiris lay in the room behind her and her aerie markings were red and black, these feet could not belong to her. Who was this Aranen, then, and how had he/she gotten in?

"They're all here." The voice lisped, confirming its owner was Aranen. It also carried the deeper timbre of a male voice.

A foot reached out and grabbed Chemel's jumpsuit by the collar. The Aranen picked her slightly up off the floor. She hung slack in his grip.

"This one's too heavy for me to carry alone, even here."

Her heart jumped. Carry her where?

The Aranen started to lower her again, but stopped. He dragged her to one side before dropping her unceremoniously. "Look at this!"

More feet moved into Chemel's range. There were four in this set, sandaled, with four hooflike claws each. Azcarn. Their owner had a little age, too, Chemel guessed. White hairs salted the dun-yellow coat.

"A treadle." The Azcarn's booming voice was male. "I noticed that the one I buried outside the entrance had been dug up."

"What if they've sent a message to DSC?" The Aranen's voice rose, shrill with fear.

"I doubt they have. The earth on this is fresh, not even dry yet, and I can see from here that the t-com hasn't been activated."

"They could have used it and then shut it down again."

"In which case, Security and Enforcement ships will

arrive in a few weeks." The Azcarn sounded unperturbed.

The Aranen's beak snapped. "Sandies! We should have come sooner!"

"We had to wait for the transport to leave. Don't panic. We're in no immediate danger from S and E. Proceed as planned."

With the Aranen muttering and snapping his beak, both intruders moved out of Chemel's sight. For what seemed like an eternity she heard them walking back and forth through the station. Doors slid open and closed. Plastic tableware rattled. What *were* they doing?

More than that, she wanted to know how they knew the location of the station and how they got in. The Niran project was no classified secret, but information on everything except the study results was restricted to keep enthusiastic amateur anthropologists off the planet.

She fought the weakness that pinned her where she lay. She had to move, to reach the t-com. At the very least, she needed to turn around so she could check on the others. Listening to their breathing was not enough. She could not distinguish among them; they were just one collective sigh blurred by the fog in her head. She shouted at them with her mind, willing them to hear. If Jiahano had any telepathic talent, she could use it now. *What happened? Are you all right?*

There was no answer.

She heard the illegals returning. Chemel flung herself back and forth inside her skull like a prisoner in a cell, beating at the immobile walls that closed her in. *Move, body, move. Run.*

The Aranen picked her feet up one at a time, lifting them to where he could catch her ankles with his wing digits. The Azcarn lifted her by the shoulders. Chemel strained to resist even a little. Instead, she hung limp in their grasp.

In her new position she still looked down, but the

added height at least allowed her to see more of the Azcarn. It answered the question of how they got in. Over his belted blanket he wore his own version of an equipment harness. A breast strap passed around his trunk in the narrow space between his upper shoulders and front legs. It was kept from slipping by a surcingle behind his front legs that connected to the breast strap at his withers. On the harness hung an electronic key.

Who did the illegals know on Center? They must have an informant. Electronic keys were commonplace, but the lock combination of the station was definitely restricted information. They might even have someone planted inside DSC itself.

The tiled floor gave way to polished stone. They were entering the hangar.

They carried her past the air scooter, which Chemel identified by the glimpse she caught of its landing runner. Then they boosted her into the sky sled. The Aranen dragged her to the back of the cargo compartment. "Why go to all this trouble of stage setting? It'd be easier just to make it look like the natives broke in and massacred them."

Chemel's heart jumped. *Massacre!*

The Azcarn chuckled. The sound came up from his chest in a thunderous rumble. "Come, now, Thiil. The *Ka'ch'ka?*" The word was three clicks, hollow ones on the ends and a sucking sound in the middle something like the tongue sound used to encourage animals. "Even a superficial investigation would tell DSC that the *Ka'ch'ka* are unlikely to massacre anyone, even *ga'aeree*. No, it's best for the study team simply to disappear without a trace. However much that may frustrate investigators, they'll come to accept it. Disappearances happen on primitive worlds all the time; most of them are never solved. Come on. The ilyein's effect won't last forever."

Their footsteps faded away across the hangar.

The cold their words left in Chemel's gut did not fade. *Disappear without a trace.* One outflung hand lay in her sight like something seen through the reverse end of a telescope. She concentrated on the distant object, straining to move it. It might as well have belonged to someone on another world. Damn her muscles. Damn the ilyein. She would *not* simply disappear without a fight—if only she were given a chance to fight.

Presently the illegals came back carrying Kiris. They laid her in front of Chemel. Now all she could see aside from her hand was a yellow wing with its red and black aerie markings. She depended more than ever on her ears. Listening, she heard the illegals make seven more trips, then the hatch of the sled's cargo compartment sliding closed. Beyond, a low rumble began—the hangar door opening.

For a moment, she was shocked. They were opening the door in broad daylight? Surely they would be seen. Then she remembered that they had already been seen, probably many times. The Shree knew quite well that these two were on Nira. She stifled her monitor's reflexes and concentrated on determining where they were being taken.

The sled banked right as it eased out of the hangar, which faced north. That meant they were heading east. Sunlight slanted in through the starboard ports, spilling more forward than port, indicating a slightly southern direction, too. Chemel pictured a map of the area and mentally drew their course across it. If she managed to escape, she wanted to be able to bring the team back to the station. Could she accomplish that without knowing the actual compass heading? And if she managed to find the general vicinity of their mountain would she recognize it?

She closed her eyes and tried to visualize the mountain. She knew the cliff face across from the observation window. That was one landmark. Then there was the bench meadow and rock face at the entrance, between two belts of trees. That was another. She tried to remember how much more of the mountain she had seen through the mechanical hawk's eyes. She had not paid much attention to it at the time.

She frowned, replaying the flight in her mind. The old mining camp site was clear. All right, that was a third landmark. Slowly, piece by piece, she built an image of the mountain. It was not complete, but rather like a computer construct from an incomplete program. Sections and detail remained missing, but she thought she had retained enough for identification.

Not until she opened her eyes again did she realize *she had moved*. More important, the action was voluntary. Slowly, she closed and opened her eyes again. She slid them from side to side. She tried frowning. Those muscles worked, too. Could the ilyein be wearing off already? She must have inhaled a very dilute dose.

Chemel did not waste time cheering. With her thoughts focused on the illegals in the pilot's compartment and the growing distance between the sled and base station, she concentrated on her visible hand, willing it to move. At first there was no response; it lay inert, palm up. Chemel set her jaw. Perspiration broke out on her forehead and upper lip. Slowly, with agonizing hesitancy, the fingers folded inward. Just as slowly, they spread again. The hand rolled at the wrist, turning its palm to the deck. When she tried to draw her arm in under her, though, it refused. Her head would not lift, either. She felt as if she were on Azcar instead of on Nira, pinned under the big planet's two gravities.

She tried again to move her arm. This time it drew up to her body, though not under her. Chemel moved one leg, then the other. The process was still agonizingly tedious; but with each passing minute, motion grew just a little easier.

Then in front of her, she saw Kiris twitch. The Aranen woman shook, stretched out her legs and the wing not folded against the deck, and rolled over onto her stomach. Kiris sat up into a squatting position and looked around, her beak half open and eyes wide in surprise.

Abrupt and complete recovery was a mark of ilyein, but Chemel was amazed to see Kiris throwing off the effects so soon. It must have something to do with her high avian metabolic rate, and perhaps the illegals had seriously underestimated the necessary dosage, which might also explain Chemel's failure to lose consciousness. She was still puzzled by her own slow recovery, unless it was a function of having gone under slower, so the recovery process was also slower.

She tried her vocal cords. "Kiris." It was hardly more than a whisper, and slurred, but intelligible.

Kiris turned her head. "What happened? Where are we?"

"There are illegals on Nira. They blew ilyein into the station to knock us out. Now they're taking us somewhere where they'll dispose of us."

Kiris stared. "Dispose—" She stood up. "Are you sure?"

Chemel tried to sit up. Not enough of her muscles were cooperating yet to manage it, so she gave up and lay panting. "I'm sure."

"But why? The penalty for intervention isn't that severe."

"Maybe whatever these illegals are doing is worth murder. I don't know. I only know what they said they were going to do."

It suddenly occurred to Chemel that she was fortunate Kiris had recovered so early. "Kiris, we're flying east and south."

Kiris tilted her head as if listening. "East by southeast."

Oh, yes . . . that precise sense of direction the Aranen had. "Do you think you can find your way back to the station? They just flew the sled out and let the hangar door close behind them, so it should be unlocked. A whistle signal ought to open it for you. Get on the t-com to Center. Tell the sandies what's happened. Tell DSC."

"What about you and the others?" Kiris frowned in concern. "I can't just leave you."

Chemel made another attempt to sit up. This time she made it. She braced herself on her arms. "You can't help us if you stay. The two of them could overpower you."

"What species?"

"Azcarn and Aranen, but—"

"Aranen?" Kiris clicked her beak. "I *can* help, then. At heart Aranen all belong to one aerie." She stepped over the bodies of her teammates to reach the pilot compartment hatch. Balling the toes of one foot, she raised it to knock.

Chemel yelped, "Kiris, don't!" Confront the illegals? That was insane.

She lunged for the Aranen woman and fell, sprawling, over Baezar.

As Kiris knocked on the hatch, she called out in a high, trilling voice, speaking an Aranen language. Chemel lay torn between the desire to haul Kiris back and to do something to insure her own safety. She did not yet have the strength to move herself much, let alone another person. The second choice was forced on her, then.

She pulled back and crouched behind Baezar, using the anthropologist's burly body for cover.

The hatch snapped open. Around Baezar's hindquarters Chemel could see Thiil in the opening. His feathers stood out so far he filled the space.

Kiris talked fast. Chemel smothered a groan. She did not understand the language, but she knew enough of Aranen vocal ranges to be aware that trilling was friendly speech. Together with Kiris's folded wings, that was enough to convince Chemel the anthropologist was taking a we-are-brothers tack with Thiil.

Thiil stepped forward out of the hatch, spreading his wings. Chemel started to shout a warning but before the words were out, Thiil had feinted toward Kiris's eyes with the free digits on one wing. As she flinched, he struck at her belly with a balled foot. Kiris doubled over and went down. Thiil swung his foot to kick her head.

Chemel willed her body to obey, and this time it did. She dived over Baezar and threw both arms around Thiil from the rear. Pinning his wings, she dragged him away from Kiris. "Kiris, are you all right?"

Thiil kicked backward, but Chemel avoided his foot. He swore in mixed Aranen and Pan, straining against her encircling arms. Her muscles trembled.

"Kiris!"

The Aranen woman folded her wings tight, pulled her legs under her, and sat up in a squat, staring at Thiil. "You hit me," she said in disbelief.

Thiil flung himself against Chemel's arms. "I'd like to break your neck."

Chemel could feel her grip weakening. She hung on grimly. "Will you go do what I told you to do?"

Kiris continued staring at Thiil, but now in horror. "You can't mean that, not to one of your own kind."

"Kiris! Roll back that cargo hatch and *get out of here!*"

With maddening slowness, Kiris stood and backed toward the outside hatch. She pulled it open with a foot. After one last uncertain look at Chemel and Thiil, she leaped out.

The air pressure in the compartment went with her, pulling Chemel and her captive toward the hatch. The tug broke her grip on Thiil. He came out of her arms whirling. One spreading wing swept at her. The blow caught her in the head and sent her falling over Jiahano. Thiil kept pivoting. When he was facing the hatch, he dived out.

"Thiil."

The Azcarn charged out of the pilot compartment to stare out the hatch after the fleeing Aranen. "Thiil!"

Chemel eyed him. If only she could overpower him,

she would have control of the sled, but how could she expect to overpower an Azcarn? Or was overpowering him necessary? Her eyes slid from his back to the open hatch of the pilot compartment.

She scrambled to her feet and raced for the hatch. The Azcarn's voice called out after her, sharp with alarm, but she did not pause or look back. She threw herself through the hatch. Feet pounded across the deck behind her. Chemel slammed the hatch shut and dropped in the lock bar.

The Azcarn thudded heavily against the other side. Chemel stood back, waiting to see what else he might do, but after that initial attack there was only silence.

Chemel started shaking. She leaned against a bulkhead with her heart hammering in her ears. She was not trained for this. Monitoring was supposed to be protecting the natives from the study team, not the study team from being attacked by outsiders.

From the other side of the hatch, the Azcarn asked nonchalantly, "How are you going to find your way back to the station?"

Chemel pushed away from the bulkhead. Her shakes were disappearing, but a heady feeling of exultation remained, like that left after the terror of a climb had gone. She headed for the pilot chairs.

The illegals had been using the chairs in the stool mode, the one best suited to their anatomy. She put up the back and arms of one from where they had been folded down out of the way, returning it to the chair mode. Then she sat down and looked over the controls.

They were set on autopilot on an altitude just high enough to clear the mountaintops. How long had it been on auto? Had they been flying a straight or curved course? If she turned in the exact opposite of the compass heading, would she end up back at the base station? She rubbed a brow tuft. If that did not work, finding the right mountain was going to be hard.

She switched on the video monitor of the cargo compartment. The Azcarn was pacing the compartment, stepping over the still forms of the team on each circuit. Occasionally he glanced toward the hatch of the pilot compartment.

Chemel tapped on the intercom. "Close the outside hatch so I can repressurize. I'm going to take us up another thousand kord."

The Azcarn hesitated, then crossed to the hatch and slid it closed.

Chemel took the sled into a long spiral climb that brought it around end for end, headed, according to the compass reading, west by northwest, back the way they had come. She wished she had some way of knowing how long they had been in the air. Since the flight clock on the control panel had not been set, she had no idea how long she should fly before starting to watch for the station's mountain.

Even though the windows of the pilot compartment offered a good view to the front and sides, she switched on the belly scanners, too. Between instrument checks and monitoring the cargo compartment, her eyes wandered to the scanner screens. After fifteen minutes she realized that what she was looking for so soon was not landmarks but some sign of Kiris. Had Thiil caught her?

Perhaps, Chemel thought, rubbing hard at a brow tuft, she should not have sent Kiris off. They could have waited until Chemel was free of the ilyein's effects. The two of them could then have gone after Thiil and this still-unnamed Azcarn. After considering that for a few guilty minutes, she decided it would not have worked. Kiris thought too kindly of people.

She glanced toward the cargo monitor again. Were the rest of them safe back there with him? He had made no threatening moves yet and did not appear to be armed. He had quit pacing and sat on a jumpstool beneath one port.

She tapped the intercom switch. "What's your name, Azcarn?"

He looked around from staring out the port. "I don't see any advantage in telling you."

"How long have we been in the air?"

He smiled and looked out the port again. Chemel switched off the intercom.

It was an interminable flight, even longer than when she lay paralyzed. Chemel kept a constant watch through the windows and on the scanner screens. The mountain could appear at any time. In the cargo compartment, Riga was beginning to twitch. Chemel hoped the Azcarn would not notice the movement.

Riga lifted her head.

Chemel doubled her fist to keep her finger off the intercom button. Warning Riga would only call attention to her. She bit at a knuckle, mentally pleading with the elec-tech.

Riga looked around slowly. Her gaze froze on the Azcarn. A moment later she eased down again and lay still.

Chemel resumed breathing, but felt no relief. More of them would be regaining consciousness soon. The next one might not be as cautious as Riga.

One of the scanner screens caught Chemel's eyes. A familiar-looking cliff slid into view. She turned up the magnification. It was not the cliff across from the station's observation window, but it was the one where the Shree had taken Prol's mechanical hawk. That meant the station was close. Chemel began studying the peaks below in earnest.

Several minutes later she found the one she wanted.

She took the sled down. The whistle signal built into the control console opened the hangar door, and once they were inside, the doors closed automatically behind them.

Chemel snapped off switches as fast as she could. Leaping from the pilot's chair, she pulled out the lock bar on the hatch and dived into the cargo compartment.

The Azcarn was tugging back the outside hatch.

Chemel launched herself at him. Her tackle sent him rolling. Together, they fell out through the half-opened hatch and crashed to the hangar floor. Chemel felt the breath explode out of her. The world went a strange hazy blue.

"Riga, help me." Her call came out in a gasp. She struggled to hang on to the Azcarn and not pass out.

Another set of feet hit the stone of the hangar floor. Hands caught at the Azcarn. When Chemel's vision cleared, they had him pinned to the floor, sitting on him, his arms twisted backward over his withers. Chemel removed his electronic key, while Riga found some cord. Then they tied his hands and, as an added precaution, hobbled his front and back legs.

The Azcarn submitted without protest or further struggle. "Do you intend to keep me bound here until the sandies come?"

His patient tone annoyed Chemel. He managed to sound as if they were spoiled children playing some unnecessarily rough game. Mouth tight, she turned back to the sled.

The other members of the team came out of their stupors one by one. Baezar and Akaara were the last, and they all wanted to know what had happened. When Chemel told them, the shocked silence was brokey only by Jiahano, chuckling.

Chemel frowned at him. She had never heard him laugh aloud before and this certainly seemed an inappropriate occasion to start. "What's so funny?"

The chuckle faded to a smile. "It is rather ironic, is it not, for them to use ilyein *against* the DSC?"

Chemel saw no humor in it at all. "We need to call Center."

"You can try," the Azcarn said.

Prol glanced quickly at him, then headed for the communications room at a lope. The rest of them followed more slowly, bringing the Azcarn with them. On the way Chemel looked into several rooms. The illegals had spent such a long time puttering around the station, she was curious to see what they had been doing. At first she saw nothing out of the ordinary.

Salah was the one to notice it. "Who laid out breakfast?"

The galley was set for a meal. There was even food in the dishes, half eaten. Tape viewers lay on tables in the commons room. Tools were spread across the bench in the electrical shop.

A chilly finger slid down Chemel's spine. It looked as if everyone had simultaneously left what he was doing and walked out. *Disappeared without a trace.*

She turned on the Azcarn. "You were going to turn us into a ghost ship!"

Every race had similar legends of towns abandoned inexplicably with meals still on the table, of ships found in perfect running order but minus their crews.

The Azcarn studied the heavy claws on his front feet.

Prol appeared in the doorway of the commons room wearing a grimace. "Bad news."

Chemel sighed. Was there anything else but bad news today? "What is it?"

"The t-com's inoperable."

Chemel frowned. "What's wrong?"

"I don't know yet."

Chemel turned on the Azcarn. "What did you do to it?"

"A few simple things. It'll take some time to repair."

"I'll start." Prol left the room.

Chemel did not want to wait. Perhaps she should take the scooter to one of the observation posts and trip the emergency pick-me-up there. She punched the computer for the map and asked for a hard copy. She caught the printout as it ran into the tray and, while she studied it, told them what she was planning.

"Do you think this is that serious?" Salah asked.

Chemel folded the map to a size she could slip into a thigh pocket of her jumpsuit. She glanced toward the

Azcarn. "It's that serious. You look after this person. I'll be back in a few hours."

"Don't leave," a lisping voice ordered.

They whirled toward the door. Thiil stood in the opening. The free digits of one wing held the grip of a needler. A digit of the other wing poised on the firing button.

"Thiil," the Azcarn began, "you don't need—"

Thiil cut him off. "I think I do. You, Virinian, untie him."

Chemel eyed him. Did the needler have anesthetic needles or explosive ones? "Where's Kiris?"

His grip on the needler tightened. "Feeding the pinna foxes. She fought when I caught her and . . . her wing broke. I left her falling."

Salah gasped. "Oh, no."

"I said untie the old one."

In the corridor behind Thiil, Prol edged stealthily forward. Chemel kept her eyes on Thiil. As Prol raised the wrench he was carrying, however, Salah's gaze focused on him. Her eyes widened.

Thiil spun. For one moment he stared in open-beaked horror at the wrench, then he fired.

Prol's chest disappeared in flying shards of flesh and bone. What was left of him slammed backward against the far side of the corridor to slide bloodily down the wall to the floor.

Chemel swallowed hard. That answered her question about the needles. She glared at Salah. "Doesn't the Lseumist philosophy permit self-defense?"

Salah recoiled. "I—" She started to cry.

Soft. Chemel turned away. She knelt to untie the Azcarn.

The Azcarn frowned at Thiil. "That wasn't necessary."

"He was going to crush my skull!"

"What was Kiris doing to you?" Chemel asked.

That was the wrong thing to say. Beyond the

needler, Thiil's eyes widened in panic. He aimed the needler at her.

"Thiil, put that thing down," the Azcarn said.

"No. No, old one. That's two deaths the sandies can charge me with, if I'm caught. It would mean ego-death." He stared at Chemel along the barrel of the needler. "So I've nothing to lose by solving our problems the one sure way."

Chapter Four

At last Salah realizes how serious the situation is, Chemel thought. She felt a pang of sympathy for the linguist. Salah looked terrified. She was even paler than usual and her plump fingers moved spasmodically, twisting together, unclasping, and twisting together again.

She was not alone in her fear. Age lines Chemel had never seen before grooved Riga's golden face, and Akaara's color had turned ash-gray. Even Jiahano had lost his remoteness. He watched Thiil with sharp-eyed attentiveness.

Time, Chemel thought. She licked her lips. She needed time to think, to look for ways out. "Thiil, you can't fly as fast as a sled. How did you get here so soon?" She was pleased at how calm her voice sounded.

Thiil snapped his beak. "I called for a ride." He spread the wing holding the needler to show her a mini-com clipped to the feathers near his shoulder joint.

So there were more than these two illegals. That did not surprise her.

She looked at the needler pointing away from her. How fast could she cross the space between them?

The needler's muzzle swung back to her. "I picked up a key and this problem solver on the way."

"It'll cause more problems than it solves." She was sweating. She could feel moisture soaking the underarms of her jumpsuit. "That mess in the corridor can't be cleaned up enough to make investigators believe we've become a ghost ship and if you just leave Prol, and us, they'll know no native weapon was used."

"Thiil, listen to me," the Azcarn interrupted.

"What more can you say? It isn't Ebre I'm doing this for now, not for my job; it's for my psyche. You've held back and mismanaged everything. I don't know why Treeth assigned you to——"

"Enough!" The Azcarn's interruption boomed like thunder.

Chemel sucked her lower lip. So the head of this group was someone named Treeth, or Ebre. She could not place either name racially, but then considering what the Aranen accent did to some names, the actual ones might not be Treeth and Ebre at all.

That was irrelevant at the moment anyway. Right now she needed an escape. The two illegals were moving toward the door to the corridor. The Azcarn talked in a low voice. Thiil hissed and snapped his beak in reply.

Watching them, Chemel became conscious of the only other door into the room, the one behind them leading into the passage up to the observation room. If only the observation room were not a dead end. Or was it? She rubbed a brow tuft thoughtfully.

The Azcarn sighed. The weary sound alarmed her. Was he about to give in to Thiil?

She slid over to Baezar. "Head for that door."

Baezar blinked. "That only goes——"

"I know. Go anyway."

He paused, then reached out to tap Jiahano's belt. The two of them eased backward. Baezar touched

Salah and Riga. Jiahano caught Sheth and Akaara's eyes.

Chemel drifted sideways until she was between Thiil and the door. She caught the edge of a plastic table. Turning it a bit with each step, she walked it with her.

Thiil finally noticed them moving. With a hiss, he took aim.

Chemel picked up the table. *"Run!"*

The six of them bolted. Holding the table before her like a shield, Chemel backed after them.

The needler's ammunition was intended for use against flesh, not plastic. So although it did not penetrate the tabletop, the force of the explosion still splintered plastic and shoved Chemel backward. She used the added momentum in her retreat.

A second needle hit the floor at her feet. Fragments of tile stung her legs. Then she was through the door. She slammed it closed.

The lock was mechanical, only token, intended mostly to indicate that the person in the observation room wanted privacy. Nonetheless, forcing it open would still take a few minutes. She twisted the lock and raced up the sloping passage after the others.

The observation room had a lock, too. She turned that as well.

"That won't keep them out for long," Riga observed.

"I know." Chemel pushed through them to the observation window. She turned open the shutters and, grabbing one, broke it out of the frame.

"Let me do that," Baezar said.

She stepped aside. He reared up on his hind legs, bringing him half a head above her, and struck at the shutters with both forefeet. The shutters splintered under his heavy claws. Then he grabbed the camouflage screening beyond the shutters and ripped it apart with one pull of his hands.

Pounding on the far door of the passage came to them like thunder.

Chemel climbed out the window just to make sure that what she had in mind would work. The cliff on each side of and below the window was marginally climbable without equipment, but over the window the rock sloped backward at a relatively easy angle. She jumped back down out of the window.

The thunder in the passage stopped in a screech of yielding plastic.

"Everyone out the window," Chemel ordered. "Sheth, you and Akaara help Baezar. I want all of you to climb above the window. Stay there until I tell you to move."

Anxious lines furrowed Akaara's scalp. "But they'll see—"

Something crashed against the outside of the door. Everyone went muddy pale. Jiahano scrambled for the window and leaned back to extend a hand to Baezar. The Azcarn leaped, clawing. With Jiahano pulling and Sheth and Akaara pushing, they maneuvered him through the window and up the cliff face. The others scrambled after him.

Chemel was last out. She did not follow the others, however. Instead, she moved to the left and down. Her soft-soled deck boots had never been designed for climbing, but she was astonished how immaterial that was with Thiil breaking into the room behind her and three hundred kord of sheer rock below. Somehow she found toeholds she could cling to.

She scuttled sideways toward a projection that hid the rest of the rock face when seen from the window. Timing was important. She must be at the projection but not beyond it before the illegals reached the window. They had to see her.

She had just reached it when she heard Thiil shout. "You keeping going," she called, as if to someone beyond her, and flattened to the rock face.

The shock wave of a small explosion slapped at her. Rock fragments like sand peppered her arm and side. She slithered on around the projection and out of

Thiil's range. They were safe from the Azcarn out here. Thiil could not climb, either, though he could always fly. He might even be able to fire the needler with his feet, but his aim would probably be poor. She fervently hoped that knowing that, he would not fly after them but go back for a vehicle. Just in case he did not, she looked about for a loose piece of rock.

"You're going out there?" she heard the Azcarn say.

"Of course. I'll locate them while you go after the scooter. We can shoot them down from the scooter."

Chemel peered around the projection. Above the window, the team hugged the rock face, their eyes enormous with fear. She gripped her piece of rock in her left hand. When she was learning to climb, she had not seen the sense in her mother's insistence that she learn to drive rock pins and throw lines with both hands. Now she was grateful for the training. As the Aranen's head came out through the window, she hurled the rock. It struck him hard on the temple. He slumped back through the window.

Chemel climbed fast, and made an equally fast lateral traverse to where the team hung on precariously with toes and fingers.

Inside the observation room, she could hear the Aranen mumbling groggily. He swore, snapping his beak. "I can walk. I can still walk." There was more mumbling, some in the Azcarn's voice, some in the Aranen's, then: "We'll both take the scooter." Their voices faded.

She pushed away from the rock face and dropped down through the window. "Come on. Hurry!" She reached out a hand to help Zeema Sheth.

They lowered Baezar back through the opening, then the rest of them followed. Chemel led the way through the smashed door down the passage to the commons room. Neither of the illegals was in sight. She peered into the corridor. Clear there, too.

"Baezar, Akaara, come help me. The rest of you get to the sled. Be careful. They may not have left yet."

She led Baezar and Akaara to Stores and handed them seven survival packs. "We may not be able to come back here again."

In the hangar, the others were already seated in the sled. While Baezar and Akaara loaded the survival packs, Chemel manually opened the hangar door and set it to stay, then she scrambled back to the sled. She found Jiahano in the copilot seat, already warming up the grids. She nodded approval. The ready lights came on as she sat down.

"Everyone hang tight!"

Reversing polarity in the grids, she pushed the steering disk all the way forward. The sled bucked, almost throwing her into the control panel, then exploded forward with a force that whipped her neck. Then it shot out of the hangar.

The cargo monitor showed the team hanging grimly to every available handhold. Chemel glanced sideways to see how Jiahano was doing and, to her envy, found him at ease, watching the instruments with detached interest.

Chemel spotted the scooter on the side scanner almost immediately. It banked toward them, indicating the illegals had seen the sled. Chemel leaned on the steering disk, her mind racing. She would have to evade them somehow. The sled could never outrun the scooter.

"Proceed into the clouds, then direct the vessel straight down." Jiahano said.

"What?" Still, she sent the sled climbing toward the nearest clouds as instructed.

"It has been my observation that most races tend to see only what lies at eye level. People on the ground generally do not notice what may exist high on walls or in the sky. Pilots pay little attention to anything very far above or below their crafts."

She frowned. "Aranens see in all directions."

"When flying . . . not when being flown."

The scooter was only a few hundred kord behind as

the sled plunged into the clouds. When the whiteness had blinded all the windows and ports, Chemel dialed the polarity of the grids back to neutral, then negative. The sled dropped as if in a gravity dive.

"How far down?" she asked.

"How low do you feel able to operate this craft?"

"I'm *able* to operate less than half a kord from the ground. I prefer much higher. Some of the natives might see us."

"Do you prefer to hide from the natives or the scooter?" Jiahano asked dryly.

At a hundred kord above the floor of the valley, Chemel brought the grids to plus-neutral and directed them backward. The sled sailed forward along the valley.

She scanned the sky overhead. There was no sign of the scooter. "Thank you, Jiahano." She touched the intercom switch. "Is everyone all right?"

None of them moved as if they had broken bones.

"In case you're wondering about our destination, it's the closer of the two observation posts. Both of them have pick-me-up signals. I plan to activate one. Then we'll try to stay hidden until a rescue ship shows up. That's the reason for the survival packs. Since we haven't opened the posts yet, they aren't stocked with supplies. We'll have to learn to live off the land.

"The Shree are diurnal so we'll hunt at night. We may be out on the planet but we're still under the non-intervention directive. We must stay hidden from the Shree as well as from the illegals."

On the cargo monitor, five faces registered disbelief. In his sand-dry voice, Sheth said, "Monitor Krar, you're unbelievable. Hasn't it occurred to you that this situation isn't covered by ordinary regulations?"

She stiffened. "We can't abandon protection of the natives simply because our own lives are in danger."

"Perhaps the Shree can help us stay alive. Salah, how fast can you learn the language?"

The linguist considered. "Since I already know the

basic phonemes, it would be just a matter of picking up present vocabulary and syntax. That should come fairly fast."

Chemel felt a chill. How could they suggest such a thing? It was totally contrary to DSC policy. The purpose of nonintervention was to avoid introducing the natives to ideas and technology beyond their comprehension, to prevent culture shock, and, more important, to allow them to evolve and grow without the negative extras that always seemed to accompany the technology given to them. Why should the Shree suffer the same hatreds, prejudices, and errors as the Sodality?

"I can't allow that. We'll have to survive by ourselves."

Sheth's scalp wrinkled. "Incredible." He executed a sinuous twist that left him on his knees. "Your desire, egg mother."

"The flight will take several hours."

She checked the overhead scanners. They looked empty. Jiahano pressed his face against the side window, looking up.

She lifted a brow tuft. "What do you see?"

"Only a Shree."

She checked the scanner again. It showed a small flying figure. At this distance there was no way to judge whether it was one of the sentient individuals or merely a wild one. She quit worrying when the creature did not appear to notice them.

The route was not one she would have preferred— winding between and around mountains, sliding the sled through valleys and passes. It made a slow flight and forced her to check her map constantly to be sure they were headed for the post. But, apparently, the route was keeping them away from the scooter.

By late in the afternoon, the terrain began to change. The sled maintained a constant altitude of one hundred kord above the ground but the altimeter wound steadily down. Around them, the mountains shortened. Instead of snow, the blunter peaks were forested. The lower slopes showed less spring greenery. Increasingly, they were browner and drier. Fewer springs glistened on their sides. As the small white disk of Nira's sun slipped down the western sky and the sled's shadow preceded them farther and farther, they emerged from the mountains, into what the Megeyn miners had christened the Firestone Territory.

The name was appropriate. Red was everywhere, from the rust-colored soil to the sheer, cave-pocked sides of sprawling mesas. The red was not uniform, but varied. It layered horizontally, obliquely, vertically . . . alternately pink, scarlet, rust, and near vermilion. The maze of mesas was interspersed at intervals with other masses of the same stone but wind-sculptured into the fantastic shapes of fairy towers and fragile bridges. Other towers were octagonal, dark basalt with white, limey crustations. In the sunset the landscape became a surreal garden, taking its color directly from the red companion sun high overhead.

Riga's voice came forward through the open hatch from the cargo compartment, exclaiming in delight.

"It's a geological formation typical of vigorous tectonic activity," Akaara said, "just like the numerous mountain chains and high level of volcanic activity."

"Are you a geologist, too?" Sheth asked.

"Oh, no. It's just odd data I've picked up programming."

Chemel was impressed by the spectacle Firestone presented, but somewhat dismayed, too. She had known the area was arid, but had not expected this much of a desert. The sandy soil supported only sparse vegetation, and that looked tough and wiry. The animal life looked no less tough and wiry. She watched, but saw no water anywhere, neither pools on the valley bottoms nor spring water leaking down the sides of the mesas. How did the animals drink down there?

At least game was plentiful. Bands of hexapodal ungulates fled before the sled, running on four legs, holding up the first pair of limbs, which appeared to be adapted for grasping. By dialing up the magnification of the belly scanners Chemel could distinguish four loosely curled toes on each forefoot.

She counted three main types of ungulates, all with coats of varying reds: a small, long-legged species with prong horns; a larger and heavier creature with a black face and spiraled horns spreading in a Y-shape; and a still larger animal with a long mane and tail and a heavy boss from which horns stretched sideways before turning forward and up. The last animal had large shoulders but only four legs. Chemel dragged their names out of her memories of briefing: fly goat, bolki—a Thajan word meaning "Y-horned"—and thunderfoot.

The hunting should be good. They might go thirsty but not hungry. They would have to be careful, though. She was seeing many Shree in the area, one every few minutes. They reminded her of Prol's mechanical hawk, playing games in the sky as the mech had. High overhead, they dived and wheeled, circling across the sky through elaborate loops.

From the cargo compartment, the team commented and speculated.

"Playful, aren't they?"

"Maybe it's a rite of spring."

"Maybe they're dancing. They have music, why not other arts?"

The sun disappeared behind the mountains. As the valley filled with shadow, Chemel switched the exterior scanners to IR mode and turned on the instrument lights.

"How far are we from the observation post?" Salah asked from the hatch to the cargo compartment.

Chemel glanced at the flight clock. "We should be there in another fifteen minutes."

She pulled the map out of her thigh pocket and

spread it on her lap where she could read it by the instrument lights. Yes, fifteen minutes at most, providing they did not run into the scooter. There had been no sign of it so far. The scanners recorded only the red light of the companion sun and blips from bodies that were so small they must be either Shree or some of the large raptor species.

Fifteen minutes. She looked forward to tripping that pick-me-up and relaxing. There was still the matter of staying hidden until rescue came, but that did not worry her right now. Activating the signal was the important step. Once that was done, it would be only a matter of time before a ship, probably a sandie cruiser, arrived. The illegals would be caught.

"Is the post inside one of those mesas?" Salah asked.

Chemel folded the map and put it on the shelf under the control panel. "It's on a basalt tower."

"They took off the top of a tower and replaced it with a module prebuilt to fit where the piece was taken out," Akaara explained.

Salah turned around, laughing. "More 'odd data' you've picked up. Is there anything you don't know about this project?"

"I don't know what plants are edible."

Food. Chemel's stomach snarled, reminding her how long ago she had last eaten. She concentrated on the instruments, ignoring her stomach. First she would trip the pick-me-up, then worry about eating. Night should be a good time for hunting. The team would have IR goggles to help them locate game, and the game would not be expecting an attack out of the dark.

The tower appeared. It lay some four or five thousand kord ahead, thrusting up from the valley floor like a pointing finger.

Chemel checked all the scanners. Clear. Not even a Shree lingered in the sky.

"I'll open the post and trip the signal," she told Jiahano. "The rest of you wait in the sled."

Jiahano nodded.

She pressed the steering disk. The tower rushed at them—three thousand kord, two thousand, one. Chemel brought up the polarity of the grids and lifted the sled above the tower. As the distance closed below a thousand kord, she cut their speed. Above the tower they halted, grids neutral. Slowly, Chemel adjusted the grids to negative. The sled settled to a feather-soft landing on top of the tower.

She stood up. "Keep the grids warm; I'll be right back."

She slipped on a pair of goggles on her way through the cargo compartment. Baezar slid open the outer hatch just enough to let her out.

On the tower, she paused to orient herself. The post diagram was clear in her mind; she had only to match it to what she saw through her goggles. All right, there was the slope like a ramp leading to a slightly higher section of stone. The entrance lay below that ramp.

The posts were not locked electronically. The builders had saved that kind of sophistication for the base station. Since the posts were little more than empty shells, the entrance had only a mechanical lock. Pressure along the edge of the door opened it.

Chemel squatted on her heels at the foot of the ramp. She felt carefully along the line where the slope met the flat surface of the lower section. Her fingers found three distinct round depressions. She pressed the one to the left, then the one to the right, and finally the one in the middle at the same time she pressed the left again. Rock shifted under her hands. A slab of "stone" lifted up before her. Beneath the former ramp surface a stairway led down into the absolute blackness of the post.

She was reaching for the hand lamp hanging on her belt when someone in the sled shouted, "Something's coming!"

She heard it—the hum of a grid drive. Her head

snapped up. Overhead, running lights outlined a sky scooter.

A voice with an Aranen's lisping accent called, "Move back from that entrance."

Chemel leaped forward.

Something hissed past her shoulder into the entrance. She reversed herself and dropped flat just as the entrance went up in a roar of heat, light, and flying stone fragments. Through the chaos in her head came one question: *how had they been found?* The rest of her mind was busy realizing that Thiil had somehow obtained something more powerful than a needler. Pure terror brought her rolling to her feet and racing through falling debris for the sled.

"Get it up!"

The sled rose. Akaara and Baezar reached out through the hatch for her, as she flung herself forward. Their fingers touched.

Thunder roared behind her. Briefly, the side of the sled glowed in a brilliant glare, then from behind, something with the force of a giant fist slammed her down against the rock. Her hands jerked loose from Baezar's and Akaara's. A million fiery needles stabbed her back. With an effort, she lifted her head and, through a haze of pain, watched the sled shoot skyward and flee to the north, the scooter behind in hot pursuit.

Chemel pressed her hands to the rock, as if pushing a steering disk. *Faster, Jiahano.*

Light flared behind the sled as the illegals fired on it. The sled wobbled in midair, then, miraculously, steadied. It kept on going.

Chemel clenched her fists. *Go . . . go!*

Both craft raced north. The sled's course twisted erratically, evasively. Could that really be Jiahano piloting through those quick turns? She cheered him on, pounding the rock with her fists.

But Thiil was not stupid. He laid down a careful, well-spaced pattern of fire. Eventually, one of the charges caught the sled full in the starboard side. The sled bucked, shook, and the next moment, its lights showed it going down. It disappeared behind a distant mesa.

Chemel held her breath. Perhaps the sled was not seriously damaged. She willed it to reappear. It did not. The scooter's lights circled for several minutes and dipped down out of sight, presently appearing heading west.

Chemel forgot the pain in her back. She sat up cursing the vanishing lights. As soon as she climbed down from this tower she was going to walk to the other observation post and trip the pick-me-up there. The sandies would hear everything she knew about these people and what they had done!

For one moment of dismay she remembered she had left the map in the sled, then she found the image of the map firm in her head. She sighed in relief.

But the feeling evaporated abruptly when she tried to stand. Her knees buckled, refusing to support her. She went down again, landing hard on knees and hands. Dazed, she wondered what this was. What was wrong with her?

Fire burned in her back. She sat down and reached back to feel what was there. Her fingers found the fabric of her jumpsuit hanging in shreds. Beneath the tatters, raw flesh recoiled screaming from her touch.

Chemel started to shake, and her anger at the illegals washed away in a cold tide of fear. She was hurt, perhaps seriously. With that realization also came a new comprehension of who she was and where she was. Alone in an alien dark on the top of a sheer rock tower, she had undetermined injuries and a dead study team. She was without supplies or anywhere to go except an empty observation post.

Her throat tightened. No, she would not cry. Salah might cry in this situation. Her broodmother certainly would, but Chemel would not. It was soft, undisciplined. She . . . would . . . not . . . cry! But still . . .

she shook. She shook so violently her teeth rattled. Overhead shone the bright ruby companion sun. Looking up at it, Chemel thought she had never felt so helpless or so alone in her entire life.

Chapter Five

It was the longest night of Chemel's life. Between the pain in her back and the unyielding hardness of the rock, sleep was impossible, even if she had dared try. Somewhere in her lurked a dark fear that to sleep now might mean never waking up again, so she sat hugging her knees and staring out into the darkness, smelling and listening to the night.

The breeze brought her a mixture of scents, sweet and musky, plant and animal, the dry odor of dust. However, almost no sound came with it. Chemel had found the dark of other worlds filled with the whirring of wings and the sharp voices of insects, with hunting calls of predators and the dying cries of their prey. Here she heard none of that, only a smothering silence in which her heart drummed loud in her ears.

For a while she cursed the illegals with white-hot hatred, but that passion was gradually extinguished through the hours of unbroken blackness and lonely silence. Looking north to where the sled had gone down, she was left, finally, with just a grim resolve to bring all possible charges against the illegals.

Having arrived at that decision, she spent the time mentally tracing the route to the other observation post and planning what she would have to do to get there. Leaving this tower was obviously the first order of business, then locating the downed sled. Depending on how hard the craft had hit, a survival pack or parts of several might still remain in useful condition. She would need to bury the dead, too. Not for a long while did it occur to her that perhaps there might be survivors, but thereafter she stared north with an intensity that made her eyes burn, frantic with impatience to know for certain.

She wished she could start for the sled now. To make certain no one was stranded in the post, the builders, Chemel knew, had cut a ladder into one of the many chimneys corrugating the sides of the tower. Even if she were able to find the right chimney tonight, however, attempting a descent in the dark would be suicidal. So she was forced to sit grinding her teeth until morning. If the first hours of the night had seemed long, the last ones were endless.

At the first graying of the eastern sky, Chemel started hunting for the ladder. Moving proved agonizing. Not only had her joints stiffened after sitting in the same position for so long, but every movement that contracted or stretched a muscle in her back brought a searing protest. Chemel ignored the pain as best she could and doggedly worked her way around the rim of the tower.

About sunrise she found the ladder, but instead of relief or satisfaction, what she felt staring down at it was sinking dismay. Fifteen hundred years of weathering had worn the edges of the notches, leaving them shallow and round-rimmed. Chemel crouched on the rim with visions of slipping from the holds and falling to her death below. The alternative to descending, unfortunately, was remaining here for Thiil or the carrion birds to find. Instead, she took a breath, blew on her hands, and slid her legs over the edge, feeling for the first foothold.

The notches had been cut on both sides of the chimney to allow the climbers to come down spread across it, a foot and a hand on each side. That way the climber's weight helped hold his feet in the notches, and he could lean against the rear of the chimney to rest. Chemel did not lean back—her nerves twitched at the very thought of touching her back to anything—but she paused every twenty kord or so, her weight first on one leg, then the other for a few minutes before continuing on.

Once, a foot slipped and dropped into the next lower notch. Both hands tore loose from their holds. She caught herself, but not before she had automatically thrown herself back into the chimney and scraped down half a kord of stone. Digging her fingers into new holds, she hung gasping and cursing, waiting for the spasms in her back to subside enough for her to continue.

The hum of a grid drive cut short her cursing. She froze in place, listening with breath held and fear washing hot and cold through her. Could that be Thiil coming back to look for her?

Desperately she looked up and down the chimney for someplace to hide, but there was nothing. The bottom was still too far away for her to hope to reach the cover there, and the chimney itself stood bare. To anyone looking in the right direction, she would be plainly visible.

A bright yellow scooter slid into sight over the tower. It circled above her, dipping toward the top of the tower then swooping down around the rim. Chemel eased back into the chimney and breathed slowly. It was all the movement she allowed herself. Without cover, her only remaining defense was immobility, in the hope she would be overlooked. But immobility was difficult; her arms and legs, aching and tired already, were beginning to tremble with the strain of holding her in one position.

The temperature climbed with the sun, heating the air and stone around her. Even the sky looked hot, its color turned copper by suspended dust. Chemel's eyes stung from sweat dripping into them from her forehead. She blinked rapidly, trying to clear them. She wanted to wipe them with a hand but did not dare.

The scooter spiraled lower down the tower. Its pass brought it within a dozen kord below Chemel, so close she could see the beaked features of the Aranen at the controls. She held her breath, hoping Jiahano had been right about people in aircraft seeing in a flat plane, praying that Thiil would not lift his eyes.

The scooter slipped on. Chemel waited but it did not reappear. Had Thiil convinced himself she was gone? She waited a few minutes longer, just to be sure, though her legs were shaking with fatigue. Finally she dared breathe freely, and then to move. She resumed the descent ignoring pain, ignoring fatigue, just climbing down the chimney as fast as she could, determined to be where she could find cover should the scooter return.

From the bottom of the chimney to the valley floor stretched a steep slope scattered with broken rock and wiry vegetation. Chemel scrambled down it and collapsed in the shadow of a large boulder to rest while she considered the next leg of her journey. A huge mesa lay across her path north—which would be quicker, walking around it or climbing and crossing it? And which would offer more cover? From seeing it from the tower she thought going across the top would, if she could manage the climb up the side.

She wiped her forehead and studied the mesa. Its lower third sloped as the base of the tower did. Above that stood a vertical cliff, but the rock face slanted back a few degrees for every ten or twelve kord it rose and a great many fissures, holes, and ledges broke the surface. While she watched, a small band of fly goats grazing on the lower slope bolted from something that startled them. They bounded up the slope as far as the rock face—and kept on going straight up!

Chemel stared. Well, if fly goats could find purchase on that rock, she should too. She would climb. She forced herself onto her feet and across the valley up the slope, grabbing clumps of brush for support when rocks and loose soil slid underfoot. All the while her ears remained tuned for the hum of a grid drive.

When she reached the cliff, however, Chemel began to wonder how the fly goats climbed it. Perhaps they *were* part fly. Even when she followed the path she remembered them taking, it required all her experience and concentration first to find and then to hang on to the holds. Where they had skipped along, she struggled, slipping and cursing. Once, when she could not find a hold at all, her sweat turned cold with fear. Then she forced the panic from her by reminding herself that the fly goats had not run out of path, and if she remained here, Thiil might find her. After a few minutes she found the foothold she needed and climbed on.

The sun was halfway to zenith when she finally crawled over the rim of the mesa. The top stretched away before her, a red plain domed in copper, covered with grass, cactus, brush, and most important, trees. Animals roamed the mesa, too, fly goats and Y-horned bolki among them. The bolki encouraged her. If they could climb up, there would have to be trails to the top somewhere. By the time she reached the far side, she might want an easy path down.

But right now what she wanted was shade and a drink of water. The sun felt like a physical blow on her back. The trees would give her shade, but what about water? Where did these animals drink?

A shadow crossed over her. Chemel dropped flat in panic. How had she missed hearing the scooter? Then she glanced up and saw what had cast the shadow. Her heartbeat steadied. It was only a Shree, not Thiil, but she must not be seen by the native, either. She stayed down, hoping her dusty jumpsuit blended with the earth.

The shadow circled Chemel twice. Insects hummed lazily in the heat and somewhere close a bird sang on a long, rising note. Chemel lay motionless, sweat prickling her, the sun burning, and the scents of dust and her own sweat sharp in her nose. Finally the shadow turned and slid away east, rippling over grass and rocks as it moved. Chemel looked after the Shree, dark against the copper sky. How she envied the being its wings right now.

Putting her hands on her knees, she pushed herself onto her feet once again. Her body cooperated with alarming reluctance and with a slight dizziness that Chemel recognized as a salt imbalance. This was dangerous. She would have to find water before she went on or she might never live to reach the sled.

She began observing the animals more closely. Many desert creatures obtained their water from the food they ate, but none of the grass or brush here looked succulent. Then she remembered the trees with the plate-sized leaves.

When she came upon the next plate-leaf tree, she reached up and squeezed a leaf between her thumb and forefinger. It gave with a mushy resistance. She pulled the leaf off the tree and tore it in two, whereupon moisture beaded along the ruptured edges. Chemel cautiously touched her tongue to the liquid. It tasted slightly acid.

Should she try eating it or not? Chemel knew of at least one dangerous plant on Nira. The sweetvine's fruit could be eaten with impunity but while fermenting the fruit juice into liquor, the Megeyn miners had also discovered that the juice became deadly poison when put in direct contact with the bloodstream. The Shree had used that property effectively against the miners. So, was this leaf safe, or a deadly trap?

She bit off a small piece and cautiously chewed it.

All her teeth could do was mash the tough skin, but the pulp between the two surfaces yielded up its moisture. When the piece had been worked dry, she waited. Nothing happened . . . no stomach pain, no nausea, no weakness. She spit out the skin with regret. The act of chewing had reminded her how long ago she had last eaten. Perhaps she could eat the pulp.

The leaf pulled apart easily. Chemel ate one side at a time, first chewing out the juice then scraping the pulp from the skin with her teeth. It tasted acid, too, like very sour citrus. At the moment, however, she did not care how sour it was; as far as she was concerned, the taste was delicious. She ate all of that leaf and then another, still checking her body responses for any sudden change. When none occurred, she tossed away caution and ate the pulp and juice of twelve leaves as fast as she could pull them apart and chew them up. Though they came nowhere near sating her appetite, she made herself stop once her dizziness and much of the fog in her head had gone. She needed to find the sled. Members of the team, people for whom she was responsible, could be lying injured and dying while she stood there.

She picked half a dozen more leaves and put them in her jumpsuit to eat later, then moved on. Exhilaration rose in her, but though she did not understand why, she did not fight it. A high could block pain, too, an effect she welcomed gladly. Swept along, she did not mind the sharp rocks under her boots, nor the sun burning down so bright her eyes smarted and felt as if they were being pushed against the rear of her skull. She felt ready to walk a hundred thousand kord.

Near the edge of the mesa she struck a game trail and, at the rim, found a clear path leading down the side. It wandered all over the rock face, switching back and forth; but following it, she reached the valley floor in just minutes. From there her path led straight north along the edge of another mesa. With luck, she thought in satisfaction, she could reach the sled by dark.

A band of bolki looked up from hunting grass to take note of her passage. Farther on, a six-legged lizard skittered across her path with an orange and brown bird in pursuit, the bird's body rocking from side to side with the pacing gait of its four legs. A whistle brought her attention to a group of eight or nine Shree flying overhead, but they were so high she did not bother to hide. She almost felt like waving at them.

Where *did* this unexpected sense of well-being come from when she did not know what she would find at the sled and Thiil might come back at any time? Was it some chemical in the plate-leaf juice? She shrugged. So be it. So be anything that would get her to the sled.

The sun set balanced on the rim of a mesa to the west when at last Chemel came around a turn in the valley and saw the sled. It lay on its starboard side at the foot of the mesa, a crumpled and twisted heap of metal. From the gouges in the slope above it, she guessed it had hit near the stone face and rolled to the valley floor. The aft end was blackened from one of the charges that hit it. With the starboard side to the ground, she could not estimate the damage done there. Nothing moved around the sled.

Chemel ran forward, climbed one of the broken runners to the hatch, and peered in. She blinked in disbelief. The cargo compartment was empty! She had expected at least a few bodies. Had the survivors taken away the dead?

Swinging over the edge of the hatch, she dropped into the sled. The bulkhead beneath her feet lay blackened and blistered, with holes burned through the metal in some places. No wonder the sled had gone down; most of the contragrav grid in that side was destroyed. Other than that, however, and the crumpling of other bulkheads, the inside looked clean. She saw only a few stains that might have been dried blood.

When she was satisfied there was nothing more to be

learned in the cargo compartment, she pulled herself up the forward bulkhead into the pilot compartment. The damage there was the worst in the ship, with all the windows shattered and the overhead caved in almost to the level of the seats. Unhooking the hand lamp from her belt, she swept the light around the compartment. Blood stained the deck and copilot chair, but even here no body was to be found. She noted that her map had disappeared from under the control panel.

Returning to the cargo compartment, she contemplated the empty rack where the survival packs had been. Not too many of the team could be injured if they were able to carry away all the packs, but how many, exactly, had survived? She did not recall seeing any graves when she approached the sled. Climbing out of the sled and scouting the area confirmed that; there were no fresh graves, not in the soft soil in the middle of the valley nor under cairns on the rocky slopes.

She rubbed a brow tuft. Could Jiahano have possibly brought the sled down without a single fatality? He would have had fewer than half his grids. Once when her mother was teaching her to fly, Chemel had had to land a scooter on half grid power. She had managed it, but only just, and that was under the most controlled circumstances possible. On the other hand, her mother had brought an experimental aircraft in on only a quarter of its grids and walked away with just bruises and a slight concussion. The evasion course Jiahano flew demonstrated he was a capable pilot, but . . . was he good enough to match her mother's feat?

Supposing they had all escaped, where were they now? Since Jiahano or someone had taken the map, perhaps they were heading for the other observation post. It lay a hundred thirty-five thousand kord northeast of the other one. If she set out after them now, she should be able to catch them in a day, or even by morning if she kept going all night.

With the valley in shadow, the temperature began

dropping. Chemel hoped it fell to freezing. That was what a proper spring night should be and it would be a relief after spending the day under Nira's sun. She was the same color as the mesa rock around her and her skin felt so hot she could have hired out as a heating unit.

Standing beside the wrecked sled, she studied the valley thoughtfully. A branch of it ran north around a mesa; another branch went east—which would the team have taken?

She circled the sled again, this time examining the ground for footprints. Too bad hunting had not been one of Athe Krar's sports! Chemel had never learned anything about tracking and was regretting that when she came upon a row of stones. It stretched east and west, beginning at the west end with a rock as large as her head and terminating six stones later with one the size of her fist.

Her heart jumped. One of them had thought to leave a marker. Who—Jiahano? Baezar, perhaps? Just in case she happened to come after them. She was grateful to whoever it was.

Straightening, she started up the valley to the east, walking quickly. She needed to use the light while she had it. Once darkness set in and she had to rely on her hand lamp to find the way, the pace would have to be much slower.

Evening proved noisier than either the night before or the day had been. From all around her came the calls of birds and animals. Dusk seemed to be a big hunting time for all of them.

Chemel became so engrossed watching the creatures that she almost passed the cairn lying some three thousand kord up the valley. In fact, she was a step past before she realized what it was. Halting in mid-stride, she whirled back. For several minutes she stood staring at it, heart dropping. Someone had been critically injured after all. Who lay under the pile of stones?

She began moving rocks at one end to find out.

What she uncovered, however, was not a body, but a survival pack. Why should they leave a pack? And what was in the rest of the cairn?

When she finished tearing apart the cairn, Chemel sat back on her heels, staring in disbelief. All the packs were there. She counted them to be sure . . . seven. Why?

The air above her thrummed. Before Chemel could move, almost before she identified the sound as the beating of wings, a Shree dropped out of the sky to land on the far side of the broken cairn.

Chemel crouched, frozen in place. For once, her mind produced a total blank, leaving her with no idea at all what to do, either with herself or with the seven packs at her feet. Her monitor's run-and-hide reflex proved of no value in this situation. She swore silently, thinking of the seven collections of tools designed to keep DSC personnel alive on alien worlds, tools now about to fall into primitive hands. She stood up and waited for the Shree to make the next move.

But it did nothing immediately, only stepped heels free of its wings and stood folding them while exchanging stares with Chemel, who noted the action with interest. So that was how their legs were free while the heels attached to the wings. It was only an in-flight attachment, an elongated bone on the heel hooking into a fold of membrane along the trailing edge of the wing. The arrangement that provided tautness in flight allowed mobility on the ground.

The Shree's dark eyes swept over Chemel in cool appraisal. Chemel replied in kind. The Shree was taller than the one she had observed through the mech's eyes. Its head reached Chemel's shoulder. Did that mean it was male? Though the thick fur in the crotch area prevented easy sex identification, something of its sleek lines and the dark honey-gold of its coat suggested a female. It also wore stone-and-carved-bead bracelets on one wrist and one ankle.

Chemel had finished studying the Shree, but the

creature continued staring at her, condescension creeping into its dark eyes. Chemel was amused. Could this primitive actually be looking down on her? Then the attitude began to disturb her. In what way did it find her lacking? Eventually, as the Shree continued to stare, Chemel really became annoyed.

"Do you mind stating your business? I have other things to do beside stand here." How ridiculous she sounded! The Shree would not understand her, which was just as well, she supposed, since she doubted her superiors would have considered it an ideal statement with which to open contact with a member of another species.

The Shree's eyes glittered in the fading light. "You be my business, *ga'aeree.*"

Chemel choked. The Shree *understood* her, and the reply—cold rage welled up in her—the reply, except for the final word, was in *Pan*! Even with a heavy accent and simplified grammar, it was still unmistakably Pan. This meant the illegals were interfering on a far greater scale than she had ever dreamed! She must reach the observation post at any cost.

She felt for a pack with the edge of her foot, covertly measuring the distance to the nearest thicket of scrub trees. The Shree were not as agile on the ground as she, nor could they take off easily once on the ground, or so the briefings had indicated. Her hope was to reach cover before the Shree could stop her. Chemel did not know why the Shree wanted her, but she had no intention of waiting around to find out.

Her heart hammered in her ears. She tensed, ready to stoop for the pack.

"Stay!" The Shree commanded, making the word two syllables with a hissing *s* and a click in place of the *t.* It pulled a knife from a scabbard on its body harness.

Chemel untensed her muscles, swearing silently.

The Shree sent a piercing whistle skyward. From

overhead came an answer. Another Shree dived over the mesa toward them, wings thrumming.

The honey-colored Shree bared its teeth at Chemel. "We be taking you with us."

Chapter Six

Where did the Shree plan to take her? Chemel eyed the two apprehensively. Were they turning her over to Thiil and the Azcarn? These people must have close ties to the illegals. And how did they think they could carry her? The trip involved flying, obviously, but though a Shree could lift eighty percent of its body weight, she weighed a good third more than either of them.

They began unwrapping long straps from their body harnesses. That answered her question of how they planned to transport her. During a briefing she had seen a tape of the Shree carrying a bolki, flying in tandem to keep their wings from tangling. The bolki hung beneath them, rear legs and a front pair hobbled with straps to give the Shree a secure grip.

Chemel's eyes widened. "No!"

She had no intention of going anywhere strung between these two. Snatching up the pack at her feet, she bolted for the nearest thicket of brush. The pack included a needler, complete with anesthetic clip. She could use it to rid herself of the Shree long enough to escape.

But she had barely started running, when something struck her hard on the back of the head. As she stumbled under the force of the blow, she recognized a rock from the cairn skittering past her. With a touch of irony, she thought of the rock she had thrown to stun Thiil. *Turnabout.* Before she could regain her balance, footsteps pounded up behind her and a spear of agony between her shoulder blades drove her to the ground.

She sorted out what must have happened a few minutes later. One of them had leaped at her and was now standing with a foot planted solidly in the middle of her back. Each time she struggled, its calloused sole scraped her raw flesh.

"Stay," the honey-colored Shree ordered.

Chemel weighed the honor of fighting against the amount of resulting pain. "All right, I'm staying."

The honey-colored Shree reached for Chemel's wrists.

Presently, Chemel wondered if the price of surrender was too high. She—a representative of an interstellar civilization, educated, a monitor—dangled beneath a pair of primitives like a hunting trophy. The straps of the hobbles cut into her wrists and ankles while her shoulders ached from the strain of her weight against them. Staring up at the companion star overhead, she could only hope the flight ended soon.

Above her, the honey-colored Shree and the other, a golden chestnut, called back and forth in clicks and whistles. Chemel worried about the survival packs. After a long conversation, which Chemel assumed was debate, and an experimental hefting of the packs, each of which weighed about half a Shree's weight, the pair had buried them under the cairn again. That made Chemel wonder if Shree instead of the study team had buried them the first time—to keep them safe until such time as they could be retrieved. Maybe what had happened to her had also happened to the team. Perhaps she would see them soon. It was a hope to hold onto.

As they started losing altitude, she twisted her head to look down over her shoulder. It was too dark to see detail any longer. The dark mass of the mesas rose from darker earth. However, light shone out through openings in the cliff face of one mesa. Her captors appeared aimed for it.

But how did they intend to land? She saw no ledge outside the largest opening and, judging from the size of the Shree standing waiting for them there, the entrance was no more than three kord wide. The Shree had a wingspan of nearly four kord. Surely her captors could not fly through that opening.

The honey-colored Shree holding Chemel's wrists kicked free of its wing membrane and dove toward the opening with wings folding, legs dangling. As the wings lost tautness, they also lost lift. The Shree plummeted ever faster for the opening. Meanwhile, the chestnut Shree kept its wings outstretched and wing fingers curved to increase the camber. Like a winged aircraft lowering flaps to increase lift while slowing down, Chemel thought.

She had only a few moments to be fascinated by the maneuver before she realized what effect the landing would have on her. Dangling lower than their feet as she was, Chemel would be dragged along the cave floor between them, *on her back*. She set her jaw, waiting for the impact.

They landed running, and Chemel hit harder than she had imagined. She also found she had not anticipated how stone would feel scraping across a back now burned as well as abraded. Only clenched teeth stopped the scream of pain rising in her throat.

Then, the motion ceased. She curled tightly on her side and sucked slow breaths through her teeth, willing the pain to subside, and hardly noticed when the hobbles were unwound.

Voices chattered excitedly. Even through pain she

noticed with surprise that most of the sounds were soft vowels and consonants, instead of clicks and whistles. She opened her eyes, and with the same care she used to breathe, she sat up.

Around her was a low-roofed cave lighted by pitcher-shaped lamps, some hanging from stone columns, others set on wooden stands. The cave smelled of the combined odors of musk, cooking, and something curiously vanillalike. Some two dozen Shree, adults and young, surrounded her.

Most wore bracelets on one or more limbs, she noticed. That eliminated jewelry as a way to distinguish the sexes. Seeing a group of them, however, she also observed that some seemed broader-hipped than others. Females? If that were so, the honey-colored Shree who captured her was a female as she had first thought, and the chestnut Shree, male.

The Shree pressed close, reaching out to touch her. As they came nearer, the vanilla odor strengthened. Their eyes glittered with curiosity.

Chemel held herself rigid to keep from flinching. Those stares reminded her uncomfortably of the Shree who had dismantled Prol's mech with such gleeful thoroughness.

The honey-colored Shree spread her wings and drove the others back. She spat something in hissing and guttural sounds. Salah would have been fascinated, Chemel reflected. Their language seemed made up of three completely different sets of sounds.

From the rear, a grizzled, iron-gray male pushed through the crowd and spoke to the honey-colored female. Chemel understood two words of the reply: *ga'aeree* and the triple-click word the Azcarn had used, *Ka'ch'ka*. A murmur ran through the group.

A reddish-tan male, regarding Chemel with bared teeth, uttered something short. The response from the Shree was sharp. Teeth bared. Some ears flattened. Wings rippled as if ready to spread. The honey-colored female turned on the red male with an angry hiss and moved closer to Chemel.

Before violence could erupt, the gray male and a black male whose coat was shedding out to silver stepped between the honey-colored female and the red male. The gray spoke sharply to them both, and the female snarled, then pulled her chin in against her neck. She stepped from in front of Chemel. The red male sidled around to the far end of the group.

Chemel rubbed a brow tuft. Now, what had that been about?

The gray Shree squatted down in front of Chemel. As he did so, the ends of his wings folded forward under him, between his legs. "What be your name?" He asked the question with a falling rather than rising note at the end.

Her normal reply—"Chemel Krar, Monitor Third Grade, Department of Surveys and Charters"—would give away too much information to these people, so she answered simply. "Chemel."

"Sh'mel," the gray Shree repeated.

Chemel shook her head. "No, Chemel . . . *ch*, not *sh*. Chemel."

"Sh'mel."

She sighed. It would have to do. "Who are you?" she asked in return.

"I be Hir'a."

Like a cheer, accent on the last syllable. Since he seemed to be someone with authority, she tried another question. "Why am I here?"

His dark eyes flickered. "She'shee brought you."

She made a note that Shree took questions literally. "I mean, why have I been brought to this place?"

"This be She'shee's band. She would not take you to strangers."

Chemel rubbed a brow tuft. Was it possible that he was playing games with her? These literal answers were also good evasions, if the Shree were capable of thinking with that much sophistication.

The honey-colored female, She'shee, murmured something that made the Shree around her hiss through their noses in laughter.

Since they looked at her while they laughed, Chemel wondered if the joke was at her expense. She pushed herself to her feet and felt better towering head and shoulders over the little primitives.

"Why did you capture me?" she asked She'shee.

She'shee's ears twitched. The eyes of the other Shree watched her expectantly. Chemel had the feeling she had made the honey-colored female uncomfortable. Good.

"The emres will not speak to us and I be curious about *ga'aeree*. What world do you come from?"

The brief speculation about who the "emres" might be ended in shocked outrage with She'shee's question. Those illegals were not even pretending to come from the far side of the world, as they could easily do. They had actually told these people about other worlds!

"I can't tell you that. It's wrong for me to be here. It's wrong for all *ga'aeree* to be on this world." She hoped she was right in assuming *ga'aeree* meant *alien*. She also hoped her pronunciation was close enough to correct for them to understand her. "I was on my way to see that all *ga'aeree* leave this world when you captured me."

"We know," the black-turning-silver male said.

The short answer chilled her. "Did one of the other *ga'aeree* tell you to capture me?"

She'shee lifted her head high. "*Ga'aeree* do not command *Ka'ch'ka*, the People."

The response had more the sound of maintaining pride than denying the question. Chemel was sure one of the illegals had asked the Shree to capture the study team. Where had the rest of the team been taken?

The Shree slowly edged closer. One of them fingered the sleeve of her jumpsuit. She wanted to back away, but there was nowhere to go. They surrounded her.

She felt as if she were suffocating. Then something touched her back. She gasped.

The Shree who had touched Chemel, a brown female shedding out tan, twitched her ears in surprise. "That hurts?" The lowered tone at the end of the question gave it the sound of a statement.

Chemel could not have agreed more. "It hurts."

"You do not act hurt."

What did they expect her to do, writhe and scream?

"I be Ibee. I have . . ." She looked at Hir'a and spoke a word.

"Healing herbs," Hir'a said.

"I have healing herbs. You wish me to use them for you?"

Chemel regarded Ibee dubiously. Herbs? Still, if it got her out of this crowd, she would submit to anything. "Use your herbs."

Ibee led the way through the cave, and Chemel looked it over with interest on the way. Caving was not one of her mother's sports, but Chemel and Klen had explored a few on their own in the mountains near their cabin. This was nothing like any of those. In fact, it looked less like a cave than like a huge cellar constructed of a series of cross-connecting barrel vaults. Thick columns stood at each corner where the vaults intersected. The spacing was much too regular to be natural. Could the Shree be capable of digging their own caves?

Ibee stopped. "Here."

It was a far cry from the quarters in the station. Nothing separated it from the rest of the cave, and the furnishings consisted of only a pile of hides on the floor next to a column and a shelf beside it. It did not appear much different from similar areas throughout the cave.

The shelf was made of animal skin stretched tight over a wooden frame. It lay supported on each end by a pile of stones. Two skin bags and some fired clay jars sat on the floor beneath it. The shelf itself held an assortment of smaller jars and some wooden and bone objects, and one polished square of what looked like pure silver. A couple of the jars, glazed in bright scarlet, seemed to be of a much better quality than the others. Chemel did not have time to examine anything more closely before Ibee pointed her toward the hides.

"Lie down."

Chemel stretched out on her stomach. The topmost hide had thick, sandy-colored hair and it was the softest surface she had felt in what seemed like eternity. Tension ran out of her, leaving instant drowsiness.

She started to close her eyes, but snapped them open again at the soft padding of feet on stone. The band was closing in around her again, watching Ibee. Chemel bit her lip. Was she that much of a curiosity?

Ibee picked an object off the shelf—a thin metal blade. Chemel forced herself to lie where she was. Still, she did not start breathing comfortably again until Ibee used it just to cut away the remains of the jumpsuit back.

The band crowded in, watching closely. Ibee reached into one of the skin bags and pulled out a handful of crushed, wet leaves. The touch of the leaves on Chemel's back sent her skin into twitching spasms, but the liquid felt cool, and after a few minutes, she began losing sensation in her back. A pleasant numbness replaced the pain.

Ibee also ran the leaves over Chemel's face and hands. The awareness of heat there disappeared, too.

"Now I wash your back."

With water from the other bag and a square of soft animal skin, Ibee proceeded to scrub. Chemel was thankful for the numbing effect of whatever that herbal liquid contained. "Where did you learn to wash out wounds?"

"Even animals lick their wounds clean," Ibee responded in a tone of surprise.

Following the scrub came a powder, liberally sprinkled and rubbed in. The hovering Shree scrutinized every movement during the procedure. Chemel wanted to yell at them, to drive them back and give herself a little room. Instead, she turned her face to the rock so she would not have to see them. Lassitude was settling over her. The pillar looked very smooth, almost glassy. Drowsily, she ran the fingers of one hand across it. How cool and slick it felt. That was her last conscious thought.

She woke some unguessable time later, still lying on her stomach. The lamp on the shelf no longer burned. Turning her head, she saw sunlight spilling in through the openings in the cliff. Morning already?

She sat up to find Ibee and a young Shree two-thirds the female's height standing beside the pile of hides. The young Shree wore what appeared to be a long strip of red fur draped around his neck . . . until the "fur" lifted its head and regarded Chemel with huge obsidian eyes. The creature must be one of the mustid burrow cats, she decided.

Ibee held out a bowl and a flat piece of something brown and crusty. "You wish to eat?"

Chemel wished. She fairly snatched the food in her eagerness. The brown piece, she discovered, was unleavened bread. The bowl held a soupy mixture of meat and unidentifiable vegetation whose aroma set her mouth watering, but the bowl itself temporarily distracted her from the demands of her stomach. Thin and light as eggshell, the bowl with its brilliant scarlet glaze reminded Chemel of the jars on the shelf.

"Where did this come from?"

"Ch'ni makes them."

Taught, no doubt, by the illegals. Was there no limit to their interference?

Someone behind Chemel asked, "How be my *ga'aeree*?"

Chemel turned to frown at She'shee. "I don't belong to you."

Ibee said, "If you be staying today, there be chores to do."

The honey-colored female stiffened. "I be flying." Turning, she stalked to the entrance and leaped out.

Ibee said, "Mind not She'shee, she feels possessive because she caught you. You belong to the whole band, though."

Chemel frowned. "I belong to myself."

Ibee's ears twitched. "The People belong to themselves, but you be only *ga'aeree*. The food satisfies you?"

Chemel sipped a bit, and jerked back as the gravy seared her tongue. "Is that why she captured me, to be a slave?"

Ibee blinked. "I do not understand this *slave*. She brought you because Shishi'ka asked it, but she wishes to have all believe she always acts as she alone wishes."

"Shishi'ka?" Chemel knew she was pronouncing it wrong, messing up the final click. "Who's that?" She tried the stew again. By this time it had cooled enough to be edible. It tasted delicious, and she drank it ravenously.

The Shree female considered Chemel's question, forehead wrinkled. "Shishi'ka be . . . himself, He Who Has Always Been."

Finishing the stew, Chemel wiped out the bowl with the bread. "You mean he's a god?"

Ibee and the young Shree blinked. "What be a god?"

Chemel tried another tack. "What does he do?"

Ibee considered. "He brings us Truth."

"What truth?"

"He told us the emres come from other worlds around the stars, and that the stars be like Z'kee, the sun. It be said that many generations ago he taught the People the *ga'aeree* tongue, so we may speak to *ga'aeree,* who cannot speak the People's tongue."

Generations ago? They thought this Shishi'ka was

immortal, then. "You really believe one person can live forever?"

"Yes," the young Shree replied.

Ibee touched the top of his head. *"Sh'sha, shishima.* This be my son Ni'in. Go to Asegah, *shishima."*

"I wish to talk to the *ga'aeree. Amma?"*

"Go to Asegah."

Ni'in sighed and shuffled away across the cave, the burrow cat still around his neck, to join a group of other young Shree and an adult lying on their stomachs in the sun near the entrance.

Chemel rubbed a brow tuft. *Shishima.* That was very close to the name of the immortal. Could the word mean *son of . . .* ? "Who is Ka?"

Ibee's eyes widened in surprise. "Ka keeps *t'k't,* of course."

There was no way Chemel could duplicate the subtle difference in the three clicks. "Keeps the what?"

"T'k't. You do not know *t'k't?"*

"No."

"I will show you." Ibee cleared the shelf and shifted it so it balanced on one of the end stones. *"T'k't."* She placed a jar at one end. The shelf started to tilt. "Not *t'k't."* She balanced it again with two smaller jars on the opposite end. "Again *t'k't."*

Oh. "Balance."

Ibee tried the word. "Balance." She lifted her chin. It was actually a double motion: lift . . . pause . . . more lift. "The universe must have *t'k't.* When too much comes to one place, too much game or too much luck, Ka adjusts."

"And you think Shishi'ka is his son?"

"Ka has no sons. Ka be not a he or a she. But Ka must be wise, *ba*? Ka be forever, also. Shishi'ka be also wise and forever."

Chemel returned the bowl to Ibee and hugged her knees. Her back felt stiff and her skin tender, but the worst of the pain had gone. "And Shishi'ka told She'shee to capture me."

Ibee sighed. The response held a note of exasperation. "He told the D'aka'reen, the clan to the east. He said there be *ga'aeree* on Ne'en who be not emres. He said they will take away the emres and destroy the People. The D'aka'reen sky-signed to us." Ibee frowned at Chemel. "Why do you wish to destroy the People?"

"I don't want to destroy them. I want to preserve them."

It sounded like the illegals had somehow learned about the Shishi'ka legend and were using it for their own benefit. But where had the legend started? Ibee said Shishi'ka taught them Pan generations ago. Had one of the previous study teams slipped past the monitor and gotten out on the planet for some fieldwork? Damn! There were more and more questions to be answered about this planet.

"In order to preserve the People, the emres have to leave. It's wrong for them to be here. It's wrong for anyone but your people to be here on your world, on Ne'en."

Ibee shook her lower shoulders. "It be good. Emres be good."

Good? Chemel sighed. What innocents these people were. "Why do you think that?"

"They dig stones out of the earth and give us some. They give us metal and blades."

Chemel wanted to spit. The interlopers had bought off the primitive natives with baubles.

"And when they finish digging, they give us the place that be left. This be much better than other caves, and there be a spring in one tunnel." She pointed to the rear of the cave. "They even cut the holes in the cliff for us."

Chemel felt as if someone had crosswired a contragrav harness she was wearing. She spun on the hides toward the glassy smoothness of the rock column. She should have known the Shree could not have built this! That fused rock had to be the product of a modern mining tunneler. If her brains had been working last night, she would immediately have recognized the origin of this cavern.

She began shaking with outrage. *Miners!*

The illegals were not only interfering with the natives, but raping the planet as well, robbing the Shree of their resources. She cursed herself for her denseness. Thiil had used the name Emre—except he pronounced it Ebre. *It isn't Emre I'm doing this for now.* Emre was the company name. Lacking a word for miners, the Shree had adopted one they heard in connection with the off-worlders. More fiercely determined than ever, she had to reach the observation post and that pick-me-up just as soon as possible. She stood up slowly and glanced around the cave. Most of the Shree there were young ones. The two adults other than Ibee appeared aged. "Where's everyone?"

"Hunting and gathering," Ibee said.

"What are they doing?" Chemel pointed at the group near the entrance.

"Asegah be teaching names."

"May I go listen?"

Ibee considered, then raised her chin in that quick double-lift motion. Chemel walked up to join the group.

The lesson was all in the Shree language. Chemel found she could understand none of it. The teacher, an old male with part of a wing missing, stopped talking as she joined them.

"Don't stop," she said.

"Tell us of your world," Asegah said. "You have what animals there?"

She sighed. "I can't tell you."

Ni'in held up the burrow cat, which hung over his hand in boneless acquiescence, tail and six legs dangling. "You have *m'im?*"

"No."

Several other young Shree had questions, too, but

when she refused to answer any of them, the crippled Shree resumed talking.

Chemel waited until their attention was once again fixed on Asegah, then eased toward the cave opening. Given a choice, she would have preferred to remain in the cool cave. The sun, near zenith in the copper sky, felt like fire on her face and hands.

She looked to both sides, then down the rock face. A nice fissure ran left and downward. The rock above it was rough, too, offering handholds. She could follow the fissure to that ledge, then climb down the shallow chimney below to that slight overhang. The overhang hid the cliff face beyond, but she felt confident the rock would provide a path.

Chemel glanced into the cave behind her. No one was looking in her direction, so she moved quickly sideways and pushed her toes into the fissure. Then she scanned the sky. Birds of various sizes flew above the mesa, but aside from them and scattered puffs of clouds, the sky was empty.

On reaching the ledge, she descended the chimney, losing some skin from her palms and elbows, but reaching the bottom safely. The overhang became a ledge she had not been able to see from the cave entrance. It led to a break in the rock face and a scree she could walk down. She moved carefully to avoid raising dust or sending rocks rolling. At the bottom, she looked around again. The cave entrances and sky were still free of Shree. Relieved, she headed for the shade of a plate-leaf tree to rest before going on.

A Shree stepped from behind the tree, and she recognized the black-going-silver male who had spoken to her the night before. *"Ha t'k't, ga'aeree,"* he said. "You be slow. I have waited two handspans passage of the sun for you."

Chemel could only stare at him.

His whistle pierced the copper sky. Ibee appeared in the cave entrance and leaped out. Her wings snapped open to catch the air.

Chemel's mind spun in hurried desperation. She had to talk fast. "Don't take me back. I'm trying to help your people, not destroy them. The emres will destroy you."

The Shree frowned. "The emres do not destroy. We want them here."

"You wouldn't if you understood that they're robbing your planet of minerals you need."

Ibee landed beside them carrying a hobble strap.

"We know what the emres be doing," the black male said. His voice was sharp.

Chemel snapped back, "You only know what this so-called Shis..i'ka tells you, but he speaks for the emres and is lying to you."

That was the wrong thing to say. With a furious hiss, the male snatched the hobble from Ibee and grabbed one of Chemel's wrists. She saw two choices: fight and lose, or submit. If she chose the first, all her movements were likely to be watched with suspicion from now on. On the other hand, surrendering might give her a chance at being trusted. She could wait for another chance to escape, and while she waited she could properly prepare herself.

She held out the other wrist toward him, too.

Chapter Seven

Chemel leaned into the grinding stone, using her shoulder and back muscles to push it through the depression of the mortar stone. Between grinder and mortar, *ch'ee'a'bae,* bitter little red berries dried hard as pebbles, became the fine powder Ibee used in wounds. Chemel worked methodically. Push . . . pull back . . . tense and push.

The morning sun at the cave mouth felt hot on her right arm and the right side of her face, but the impatient racing of her mind blocked out any discomfort. She swore silently. Here she sat, housekeeping, while the people she was responsible for remained lost somewhere out there. The Shree knew what had happened to the team, or could find out, but they would not even discuss it. Meanwhile mining crews were stripping away at the planet. Her frustration at her impotence made her want to pound her fists bloody against the cave's stone. Instead, she dug her fingers into the grinding stone and rammed it hard into the mortar. Push . . . pull . . . push.

She scraped the powder into the herb jar and spread more berries in the mortar. One berry she slipped into the pocket of her shirt. Tonight it would join twenty others in the skin bag under the thunderfoot hide she slept on, marking one more day lost with the Sun Cliff band.

Lost was not quite true, perhaps. She learned more all the time about the Shree, their language, and the Firestone Territory. She had sewn a hooded shirt and trousers of bolki skin. They were soft to wear and loose enough to be cool, but resistant to rock scrapes and thorn tears. She was making sandals, too, though if she continued to run barefooted as she was now, her feet might be so calloused by the time she left that she would have no need of them. She also knew where the parts of at least one survival pack were.

When Ia'hi, the black-going-silver male, brought in the pack the afternoon after she was captured, he had spread the contents before her. "What be these things?"

She evaded. "Where are the other packs?"

"Given to other bands, keeping *t'k't.*"

While she watched, he paged through the manual. He skipped the text, but studied every diagram closely. To her amazement and dismay, he used the manual to help him assemble the collapsible shovel. He then passed the shovel to Hir'a. From Hir'a it went to every member of the band, to be held and worked.

The protein analyzer defeated him, remaining an inert tube in his hands. After a bit, he laid it aside with the rope. Then he picked up the needler.

Chemel had held her breath.

The weapon looked huge in his small hands, but he handled it with confidence. She decided he must have seen miners use needlers. She was relieved to see that he kept his finger off the firing button and that only the adults were allowed to hold the weapon when it went around the circle.

The compass fascinated them, and they learned to operate the sparker after only a few tries.

When Ia'hi opened the drug kit, Chemel broke her resolve to say nothing. "Don't touch those."

He pulled his finger back from the vial he started to prod. "What be they?"

"They're like Ibee's herbs, but much stronger. They can kill you if you don't know how to use them."

At that point, Ia'hi closed the kit and did not pass it around.

The tool kit went around, though, and when everyone had seen everything, Ia'hi took the needler and drugs, then let the band divide the rest among them. Chemel carefully noted just who took which of the most important items. Me'a'na had the sparker; Bi'nrar, the knife; G'han, the compass; Ibee, the shovel. She'shee asked for the manual. Ch'ni had the pack itself and Asegah, the rope.

In case she could not reach the rope, she had begun braiding a thunderfoot hide in one of the unused galleries at the rear of the cave. She had the time. Property they might consider her, but not a slave. As soon as she finished the chores set for her, tasks usually given to band members too young, old, or crippled to fly hunting and gathering, she was free to do as she wished within the cave.

The only problem was doing something without twenty-two adult and young Shree looking over her shoulder. No matter what was happening, they all wanted to be in on it.

Chemel stopped grinding and sat back on her calves. She stretched, working the kinks out of her shoulders. Opposite her in the entrance, Hib'aki, a young, amber-eyed female, whose summer coat was the same cream-tan as Chemel's shirt and trousers, looked up from where she squatted beside her mortar grinding grain into flour. Her forehead furrowed. "Be all *ga'aeree* silent as you?"

Chemel blinked. "What?"

"You have not spoken a word in three handspans." Her voice, as small and delicate as Hib'aki herself, drooped in disappointment and hurt. "You will not even speak back when I talk to you."

Guilt pricked Chemel. She might refuse to answer questions but she should not ignore Hib'aki. She was one of the friendliest adults, and the least condescending.

"I'm sorry, I was thinking."

Hib'aki shifted position to change the weight of her belly, huge in advanced pregnancy. She squatted with knees together to bear the weight of her belly, but kept her ankles spread so her wings could curl forward under her. The position looked horribly uncomfortable to Chemel, though she had seen Hib'aki maintain it for hours at a time.

"Thinking what?" Hib'aki asked.

Wryly, Chemel reflected she should have expected that. What did she say now? She could hardly admit she was thinking about escape. "I was thinking about all those names Asegah teaches the young ones. Why are there so many? A tree can't have just one name, it seems. The leaves have another name and the roots, another yet. Every mesa and valley has a name, too."

"They must have the names, so I can say to another, 'I must have *kar'ara* root. There be some at Three Trees Valley.' They go to Three Trees Valley and find the *kar'ara* root."

Chemel saw the logic in that. No wonder the young Shree spent so much time learning names.

She picked up the grinding stone again. Push . . . pull . . . push. With every push came another question. How was Emre hiding this planet? How was it keeping its crews from talking about the planet when they finished their duty tour here? Where were they selling the ores they took out? Surely they had to list origins on all flights. But most important of all, where were the other study team members?

Hib'aki cried out.

Chemel looked up. "Are you having pains?"

Hib'aki shook her lower shoulders and pointed south. "Flasher."

A brilliant point of light like a miniature sun flared in the copper sky. That would be the sun reflecting off the polished piece of silver every flyer carried.

Hib'aki picked up a similar piece lying beside the cave entrance and sent back an answering flash. "Now comes the sky signing."

The light flared again. This time it remained, albeit flickeringly, and moved through a complex pattern of loops. The pattern meant nothing to Chemel, but she watched along with Hib'aki. She was impressed by the skill it must take to keep the flasher pointed at the sun while flying the pattern, and to make the loops exactly right. A wrong turn or a circle of the wrong size changed the entire meaning of the message.

The first time sky signing had been explained to her, Chemel thought of the Shree flying the day the sled ran for the observation post, and she had understood how the illegals knew where to find them. Thiil or the Azcarn spoke to a Shree and from there the message to watch for the sled went out across the inhabited area of the planet, traveling farther and faster than the sled could ever hope to.

"The hunters met two wanderers. They be coming home with the hunters." Hib'aki turned to shout the news back in to the cave in clicks and whistles.

Why the excitement? "What are wanderers?" Nomads, perhaps? That must be unusual, if so. She understood Shree were firmly territorial.

"All males must leave their mothers at manhood to hunt for a new band."

Oh, so it was the males who moved while the females held the territory. No wonder Hib'aki was excited. If they enticed the wanderers into staying, the band would acquire two more hunters, and maybe a mate for She'shee.

Everyone in the cave rushed forward to the en-

trance, all talking at once. Only a young female near-
ing puberty said nothing, but stared off to the south,
dreamy-eyed.

Me'a'na said, "We will need more flour for bread.
Ga'aeree, you help with that."

Chemel cleaned the *ch'ee'a'bae* powder out of her
mortar and poured in grain. Wanderers. How far did
they wander? She wondered if it were possible they had
seen other *ga'aeree,* or at least heard something of
them.

She waited impatiently the rest of the morning. Reflexes carried her through the chores that needed doing: shaking out sleeping hides, sweeping the cave with
a brush made of a thunderfoot's tail, setting the night
jars in the entrance for someone with wings to carry off
to dump the fecal material. The urine she poured off
into storage jars where it was saved for curing hides.

Every few minutes she glanced out the entrance at
the southern sky. Near noon she saw flyers, but there
were only three, Ibee, Ch'ni, and Ala'ka back from
gathering roots and cactus. The hunters did not appear
for several more hours, and then it was Fis'isa,
Hib'aki's daughter, who saw them first. Her cry
brought everyone running to the entrance. Eight flyers
hung silhouetted against the copper sky, the six hunters
from the band, including She'shee, and the two visitors.
All the shapes looked bloated and flew sluggishly.

Ia'hi came in first. Chemel instantly saw why he
looked bloated. He wore his load of the already-butch-
ered kill strapped to his body harness. He approached
high, wings stretched to full extension and steeply cam-
bered. Almost at the rock face, he let himself float
down toward the cave entrance. At the last possible
moment, he folded his wings and stepped onto the
rock. When he was safely inside, he kicked his heels
free.

In the process of landing, he had almost fallen into
the welcoming committee. His wings snapped angrily
open again and he held his spear high, where it could

not strike anyone. He snarled at them. "Get back! We be carrying full loads. Back, *ga'aeree*." He bared his teeth at Chemel.

Hir'a was next. She'shee, Ra'ab—the chestnut who had helped capture her—then Bi'nrar and G'han. G'han eyed her hostilely as he came in. Chemel paid little attention. G'han did not like *ga'aeree*. He was the red Shree who upset everyone the night she was brought in. His suggestion, she learned later, was that if she were a danger, she should be left out where a tiger wolf or black-back cat would find her.

The first visitor to land was the tallest, thinnest Shree Chemel had yet seen, a good one and a half kord. He held out hands palm up and open in greeting. *"Ha t'k't.* I be S's'lis. I—"

He was interrupted by a shrill whistle/click combination of danger. He looked back over his shoulder, then with a yelp of dismay, dived to one side, shoving members of the band with him.

The second visitor arrived in full flight. Chemel gasped along with everyone else. Surely he was going to kill or cripple himself, as he could not possibly stop in time to avoid striking the cliff at the speed he was approaching, and the opening was too narrow for a flying entrance. Five kord from the entrance, the visitor suddenly rolled ninety degrees, so that his wings were vertical. He sailed through the entrance, just brushing floor and top with his wingtips. Inside, with Shree scrambling to avoid fouling him, he righted himself, snapped his wings closed, and came to a standing landing.

He looked around with eyes like black fire. For a moment Chemel felt she knew him, then she realized why. His eyes had the same mad shine her mother's did.

"I be Ch'ae," he said. He looked at She'shee.

She'shee's upper lip pulled back from her teeth in scorn. *"Shishima."*

The visitor seemed undisturbed. He loosened the

straps that held his burden and set it on the floor, then turned to greet the entire band. As he did, Chemel saw patches of white in the copper hair on his back.

Ia'hi hissed at him in the Shree language. Hir'a spoke more softly, but with no less emphasis. And Chemel saw with amusement that Me'a'na's youngest daughter, the one just reaching puberty, stared at Ch'ae with shining eyes. The young female continued watching him long after his daredevil entrance had been forgotten in the business of examining what the hunters had brought back.

"We killed a *t'kan'dan*," Ia'hi said.

Chemel could see the thunderfoot's hide there, part of the load Ra'ab carried. There did not seem to be enough meat for a thunderfoot, though. She saw no more than the usual four-day supply. "Where's the rest of the meat?" she asked.

Ibee's ears twitched. "They would not bring it *all* home, *ga'aeree*. It be too much. *T'k't* would be disturbed."

Oh, yes. Keep the Balance, as their greeting said, because if one did not, Ka would be around to adjust it, and Ka, inexorable, unentreatable, might adjust in ways the Sun Cliff band would not like.

"What did they do with the rest?"

"We gave it to the Shadow Mesa band, of course," Ia'hi responded, impatiently. "Their youngest hunters be injured now and the rest be too old to hunt well. Help me carry these."

Chemel wanted desperately to talk to the visitors, but Ia'hi thrust the bloody quarter at her. She took it gingerly, holding it out away from her in an attempt to keep the blood off her shirt. He picked up more meat, with less care, and led the way back to the cool storage area. Four *m'im* followed, licking up the drops of blood from the stone.

Once the meat was stored, Chemel headed back for the front of the cave, only to be sidetracked to help cook the meal. She shrugged. She would talk to them later, while eating.

Like all meals, when ready, the food was put down on the floor in its cooking containers, fired clay pots glazed scarlet and one treasured metal pot of Me'a'na's that had come from a mountain band. Everyone squatted around the pots, wings tucked neatly forward beneath them, and dipped in with personal bowls, fingers, or pieces of bread.

Chemel ate with them as always, but she still found no chance to talk to the visitors. The band wanted to know all about them, too. They all spoke in the Shree language but when asked, Hib'aki translated for Chemel.

One question was how Ch'ae had come to acquire the white patches on his back.

Ch'ae sat up, eyes snapping. "I got them when I earned my name Eagle. I be five Passes old." Chemel translated that into ten standard years. "My wings be grown enough for me to fly. One day an eagle saw me and wanted me to feed her young. She attacked me." He struck forward with both hands, fingers spread like talons. "She caught my back with her talons. The pain be terrible. I screamed and fought."

He shrieked to demonstrate and fell back writhing. The young Shree squealed in sympathy.

Ch'ae came back up into a squat. "I thought I would die. Then I had an idea. We came to a stream of . . ."

Hib'aki could not translate the word. "It be a kind of air. You have no word for it."

"I flapped my wings and flew up into an inside loop. The eagle and I then be upside down. The eagle tried to right us again but I flapped my wings harder and kept us upside down. We started to fall."

His young audience covered their eyes. "No, no."

"The eagle became afraid. She let me go. When she did, I slipped over again. I grabbed her." He grabbed, snatching at the air. "I broke her neck. And that," he said, looking at She'shee, "be how I earned my name and these scars."

She'shee looked the other direction.

Ch'ae asked a question that Hib'aki did not translate. Chemel understood a few of the words, though. From those, she guessed the rest. She thought Ch'ae was asking, "You doubt I can fly upside down?"

Ch'ae stood up and pointed at the entrance, speaking. The entire band jumped to its feet with excited clicks and whistles, then headed for the entrance.

The sun had just set. The valley was in shadow, though plenty of light remained in the sky. Ch'ae jumped from the entrance. He fell a few kord before opening his wings to catch the air. Once flying, he climbed, looping on the way up.

Someone whistled.

Ch'ae whistled and clicked back, then rolled forward into a midair somersault and headed back toward them flying upside down.

The band whistled approval.

Ch'ae rolled over one wingtip back into normal flight. He called, "Wing dance."

Hir'a leaped out. The two fell into patterns like a miniature sky sign, flying intricate loops around each other. For an aging hunter, Hir'a still moved with surprising grace and agility. In another few minutes, most of the band were in the air.

Asegah and Hib'aki brought out a wooden flute and a set of click sticks. The four click sticks, two hollow, two solid, made three sounds, dependng on which combination of two were struck together. Hib'aki produced rhythm with the sticks and Asegah improvised a melody on the flute. As the flyers fell into time with the music, the air filled with the harmonizing thrum of over a dozen pairs of wings carrying their owners through intertwining passes and loops.

Since she had been with the band, Chemel had seen numerous wing dances, but each one always amazed her. How could so many fly so fast and so close, yet never collide?

The Shree scattered about on the cliff clapped and sang along with the music. All but G'han. Chemel saw him on the little ledge outside the next opening. Instead of watching the wing dancers, he looked at her. After a long, insolent stare, he turned away.

Chemel rubbed a brow tuft. He usually ignored her. Why the sudden interest this evening? Perhaps she should try to find out.

She went looking for Ibee's son. She found Ni'in several entrances down, standing with his *m'im* draped around his neck. She bent down next to his ear.

"G'han knows some kind of secret about me. See if you can find out what it is without letting him know what you're after."

That kind of challenge was too much for the young Shree to resist. In a few minutes she saw Ni'in sidle up to G'han and start chattering. Beyond them, she saw something that interested her even more—the visitor S's'lis leaving the dance. She strolled down the cave toward him. "I'm Chemel."

He looked around at her. "A *ga'aeree*. What be your world?"

"We call it the World. How long have you been a wanderer?"

He waved his wings slightly, setting up a cool current Chemel found wonderful. "One Pass."

"Do you travel very far?"

His chin came up in a double lift. "We have gone east to the Great Cliff and north and south to the mountains where there be no people, only *z'z'ras*."

The Great Cliff would be the Firestone Escarpment, a two-hundred-kord wall of rock plunging down to the Tuka Plain. And they had been north and south to the edges of the civilized world. "What are *z'z'ras*?" She managed the whistle syllables.

His ears twitched in surprise. "The wild ones, those who look like the People but have only animal minds." His ears pricked toward her. "What be your world like?"

She pretended not to hear his question. "Have you traveled very far in the last twenty days?"

He could ignore questions, too. "Why be *ga'aeree* so different from each other?"

Chemel stopped breathing. She resumed with caution. "Have you seen other *ga'aeree* recently?"

S's'lis became interested in folding his wings properly. He spread and resettled them several times. "I have seen emres. They be *ga'aeree.*"

That was true, but she had never heard a miner called anything but an emre. She leaned down so she could be on a level with his eyes. "The *ga'aeree* Shishi'ka wanted captured are people I'm supposed to care for. I need to know where they are. Have you seen another *ga'aeree* in the last twenty days? Tell me if he or she was well."

S's'lis looked around as though seeking escape. "I do not know when a *ga'aeree* be well."

"Then you've seen one? Where?"

S's'lis frowned. "I did not say I had seen any *ga'aeree.*"

"I know—"

"Enough," a sharp voice interrupted. Chemel looked around into Ia'hi's eyes. His ears lay flat against his head. "Shishi'ka wishes the *ga'aeree* to be held in secret. They will be held in secret."

She glanced around. One or two of the band, young ones, were looking at them, but most attention remained on the wing dance. She lowered her voice. "Why do you care so much about what Shiski'ka wishes? Don't the People belong to themselves?"

"We honor Asegah and Me'a'na for the wisdom of their age," Ia'hi snapped. "How much more we should honor one who has lived forever."

"Old isn't necessarily wise. Also"—she braced in case the blasphemy she was about to utter provoked violence—"how do you know this one who calls himself

Shishi'ka is really the same one your foremothers knew?"

S's'lis stared, too shocked for speech. Ia'hi drew his upper lip back in a snarl—then relaxed his lip and frowned in thought.

Chemel tossed in another argument for him to chew on. "You've never said what he looks like but he isn't *Ka'ch'ka,* is he? That means he's *ga'aeree*. Do you bow to the wishes of a *ga'aeree*?"

S's'lis sputtered. Ia'hi put a hand over the visitor's mouth. "S's'lis, you will say nothing of this. I must think on it."

He turned and disappeared into the growing dark in the cave. Presently, Chemel saw a spark jump, and the flame of a lamp appeared in Ia'hi's sleeping area. S's'lis backed away from her.

At the cave entrance, the music had stopped. In a thrum of wings and chatter of voices, the wing dancers came back to the cave. Chemel glanced out. It was too dark for safe flying now, but that would not be the end of the evening. A handful might still have enough energy to foot dance, and certainly the music would go on. Or perhaps they would tell stories. She moved toward the circle forming inside the ring of lamps Ala'ka was lighting.

S's'lis ran a finger down the edge of Hib'aki's wing. The little female looked around, listened, then with a double lift of her chin, handed him the click sticks. S's'lis squatted and arranged the sticks on his wingtips. He began to play.

Chemel was no expert on Shree music, but she could tell S's'lis had a sense of rhythm. The sticks danced in his hands and sang against each other. He soon had everyone bobbing in time to the sound. Asegah struggled for a bit to improvise a tune to go with them, but gave up. He let S's'lis play on alone.

The sticks caught at Chemel, too. Her pulse leaped in time to them. The beat was so hypnotic she did not notice the stroking on her trouser leg for some time.

"Ga'aeree," a small voice whispered.

She smelled the strong, musky odor of *m'im* and looked down.

Ni'in's eyes glittered in the lamplight. He pulled on her wrist.

She knelt beside him. "Did you find out the secret?"

His chin lifted. "The emres be looking for *ga'aeree.* G'han saw sky signing. They will trade blades and spear points for them."

Cold washed through her. She was not surprised they were looking for the team. They would have checked the sled by daylight, too, and found it empty. What filled her with fear was the price they offered. Putting a knife and spear point against the mysterious Shishi'ka's wishes, which would influence the Shree more?

"You tell me a secret now," Ni'in said. "What be your world?"

She looked at him for a moment. Well, why not? It was a fair exchange. "It's called Virini. It would seem very cold to you. There are large oceans on it and strip continents with many mountains in the interiors. Don't tell anyone else what I'm telling you."

He shook his lower shoulders.

She stood up, biting her lip. G'han disliked *ga'aeree.* How long would it be before he could not resist trading her for something really useful to him? She had better watch for an opportunity to escape, and hope it came soon.

Chapter Eight

The visitors stayed on at the invitation of the band. Chemel suspected it was really She'shee they stayed for. Every day more of the honey-colored winter hair shed out and her summer coat appeared: sleek, silky, a gold so clear it glowed, accented by the black of her eyes and wing membrane. Even Chemel could appreciate what a beauty She'shee was by Shree standards. The visitors were besotted with her.

They vied endlessly for her attention, singing, flying, telling witty stories and recounting hunting exploits. All in vain. She'shee ignored them. When she did have a comment, it was usually the same, delivered in an unvarying tone of scorn: *"Shishima."* Chemel began to feel sorry for the two young males.

Chemel was not a willing witness to the courting, but she had nothing else to do, no work she could plead as an excuse to escape. There was enough meat and roots for four days, enough grain ground for bread. Except for dumping the night jars and preparing one meal each day, no one in the band had any required chores.

Today most of the adults had taken the young ones out for field experience naming plants and animals. Asegah sat in an entrance working on a new body harness for someone. This one was black, colored by some vegetable dye Me'a'na had discovered during the winter. Hib'aki puttered in the cooking area, boiling, shredding, crushing a plant someone brought in, doing everything she could think with it to find what it might be useful for. Of the flyers, only She'shee had elected to stay home, which meant S's'lis and Ch'ae remained behind as well. She'shee had decided she wanted to draw a portrait of Chemel.

Chemel thought of her thunderfoot rope, and of G'han and of the price on her head. She pleaded the necessity of time by herself.

But She'shee would have none of it. "If I can make a picture that looks like you, then I can make pictures of plants and animals. We can show the young ones what they look like even when it be not the season for them."

"Can't you draw one of them?" Chemel pointed to the visitors.

S's'lis and Ch'ae brightened hopefully.

"I want you." She'shee pointed at a spot inside one of the small entrances. "Sit your strange way."

With a sigh, Chemel kneeled down and sat back on her lower legs. S's'lis tried to imitate her, but gave up after a minute when the position splayed his wings out at an uncomfortable angle that made him wince. He stretched out on his stomach instead.

She'shee squatted, using her knees to support her "canvas," a sheet of stiff hide stretched over a wooden frame. She picked up a stylus made from a smoothed sliver of bone. After squinting at Chemel for a minute, she dipped the pointed end of her stylus into a small jar of ink and drew it across the taut hide.

"Where did you get the idea to do this?" Chemel asked.

"The thing from the pack." She pantomimed turning pages.

The manual had given her this idea? "How did it do that?" Chemel turned her head to look at She'shee.

"Do not move."

Chemel turned back.

She'shee dipped her stylus again. "If *ga'aeree* can make pictures that teach Ia'hi how to put the digger tool together, the People can make pictures to teach the young ones the shapes that go with the names."

She had worked all that out just from watching Ia'hi? Chemel ticked her tongue against her teeth. This demonstrated how almost anything could influence another being's thinking. She wished every Sodality citizen and artifact were a hundred light-years from Ne'en.

Ch'ae squatted with his wings to the cave wall, watching She'shee longingly. In Pan, he said, *"Ga'aeree* be better pets than *z'z'ras."*

She'shee frowned at her stylus. Chemel could guess why. She'shee had to dip it every few seconds. A brush would have been better, or even a pen made from a feather. Chemel bit her tongue to keep from telling the Shree.

"There be a female named H'nem of the Mountain-in-the-Mist band who found a young *z'z'ras,"* Ch'ae said. "She made him a pet. One afternoon when he be grown she be alone in the cave with him. The hunters came back to find her——"

Without looking at him, She'shee said acidly, "I be not interested in perversion, not even told in the *ga'aeree* tongue."

Ch'ae's ears drooped. Chemel fought down a giggle. He looked so disappointed. No doubt he had been about to recount in enthusiastic, explicit, and salacious detail what H'nem and her pet wild Shree were doing. That surprised her, and then she wondered why she was surprised that the Shree had taboos and dirty stories like every other race she had ever met. She supposed it was because they were primitives, and being a young race, she somehow thought of them as innocent, like children.

Impulsively, to cheer the visitor up, Chemel urged, "Tell us another story."

"Tell the story of Ch'be," S's'lis said.

"What's Ch'be?" Chemel thought she had managed the sucking click pretty well.

"The red star." Ch'ae looked at She'shee with a malicious glint in his eyes. "She Who Will Not Be Mated."

A flick of her ears was the only indication She'shee gave of having heard.

Ch'ae stood up to give himself room for gestures. "Once in the youth of Ne'en, the mountains be not rooted to the earth as they be now. Then they flew even as the People fly. The most beautiful and graceful of all be a red mountain named Ch'be. One day Z'kee, the sun, noticed her and began to desire her for his mate. He stayed longer in the sky every day to watch her until finally night disappeared.

"Ka came to see why *t'k't* was wrong. Because he be afraid how Ka might adjust *t'k't*, Z'kee tried to kidnap Ch'be before Ka could arrive. She slipped away from him and ran." Ch'ae lunged forward, grabbing the air, then spread his wings to become the fleeing Ch'be.

She'shee ducked a sweeping wing, hissing.

Lost in his story, Ch'ae was oblivious to her displeasure. "Ka arrived. Ka looked at Ne'en and ruled that all the mountains must stop flying. As each mountain came down to rest, Ka rooted it in the ground. The mountains struggled." Ch'ae grabbed hold of each of his legs in turn and pulled up as though to jerk them from the rock. "But Ka be too swift and too strong. The mountain be held fast. Once in a while, a mountain still remembers its young days and the whole world shakes as it tries to pull loose.

"Finally, only Ch'be still flew, and she could not rest because she be running from Z'kee. Ka saw that while

Z'kee chased Ch'be he went around the sky and there be night and day. Ka decreed that Ch'be must run forever.

"She be faster than he. When she be farther ahead, he runs faster to catch up. The days become shorter. When Ch'be be very far ahead, she rests in the night sky, hidden from Z'kee by Ne'en."

Chemel nodded. The red star shone in the night sky all winter.

"But since she be faster than Z'kee, she catches up to him. He slows down to wait for her and the days become long. He grows hot with desire. But always, when he grabs for her"—he lunged forward again, once again being the sun—"she ducks around behind him and runs away again." Ch'ae sighed. "Poor Z'kee. No matter how much his desire and how hard he strives, Z'kee can never have Ch'be."

"There be a lesson there," S's'lis murmured. He and Ch'ae exchanged wry looks.

"It's a good story," Chemel said.

She'shee sniffed. "For *shishima* and savages. The mountains never flew. Ch'be be a burning ball of gas like Z'kee, but smaller and farther away."

Chemel's mouth tightened. They were slowly being robbed of even their legends by the miners' interference. The more she saw and heard, the stronger she felt the necessity of jerking everything alien off Ne'en—yet there she sat, helpless, doing nothing more constructive than posing for a portrait. She swore silently.

A howl of pain from the cooking area interrupted her thoughts. Chemel's head snapped around. Hib'aki was wheeling around the stove oven, holding one hand and screaming.

From where he squatted working on the harness, Asegah hurried to her. The Shree with Chemel also jumped to their feet and ran to comfort her. Chemel came close enough behind to step on their wingtips.

Along with them, she examined the burned hand. It looked like a minor injury, not worth such noise.

"Put it in cold water."

Hib'aki's shrieks did not stop. The Shree stroked her head and wings. They blew on the burn and murmured soft Shree words.

Chemel stepped back, frowning. "Does it really hurt that much?"

Asegah looked around. He pulled in his chin. "To be comforted when hurt, it be necessary to act hurt."

You do not act hurt, Ibee had said looking at her back the night she was captured.

Suddenly Hib'aki stopped screaming and clutched at her belly, eyes widening.

Quickly, She'shee asked a question.

Hib'aki replied. She waited several minutes, then shook her shoulders. She licked at her hand and turned back to the boiling water as if nothing had ever happened.

Inspiration struck Chemel. Now she knew the best time to escape. If she were learning anything about the Shree at all it was that they did not want to miss any excitement. When Hib'aki's labor began, the entire band would be so intent on watching the process no one would pay any attention to a *ga'aeree*. The opportunity should come soon, too.

She'shee pointed to the entrance. "Sit again."

Chemel sat, but this time she did not mind. She occupied herself going over and over what she was going to do, mentally rehearsing her escape.

The shadow she cast had reached to where S's'lis lay when She'shee finally gave her permission to move. Chemel walked over to see the portrait.

The result was better than she expected, though not very flattering. Surely her cheekbones were not that prominent nor her nose so sharp, nor her ears so flat against her head. What did impress her was the detail. The stylus drew very fine lines, enabling She'shee to create Chemel's brow tufts and lashes hair by hair.

"This isn't your first try at this, is it?"

"I have done it before, but never to make a picture for a lesson." She'shee considered the drawing, looking from it to Chemel. She frowned. "It needs colors."

Wings thrummed in the sky outside.

S's'lis looked out. "They be bringing the young ones back."

The flying young Shree were first, then the adults carrying the nonflying young. The young ones rushed in all talking simultaneously. Their voices reverberated off the walls of the cave until there seemed to be a hundred of them. Heat from the flyers eddied around Chemel, as did a sharp, spicy odor. The roots protruding from the harness pouches of several adults told her the source of the odor. The group seemed smaller than it ought to be, though. Chemel counted heads and found Ia'hi and Hir'a missing.

The band spread out across the cave, stripping off harnesses, some stretching and waving wings to cool off.

Me'a'na pointed at Chemel. "*Ga'aeree*, help me."

She put Chemel to work washing and cutting up the roots brought back. Their spicy odor quickly filled the cave. A little was all right, but this much became overwhelming. Chemel wondered how long her hands would reek of the roots.

Light flashed at the cave entrance. "Ia'hi and Hir'a be coming," a young Shree cried.

There was the usual rush for the entrance. Chemel joined. Overhead, the two flying figures carried something slung between them.

"Hunting?" someone asked.

The object did not have the shape of an animal, though. Chemel saw no hanging head or third pair of legs.

Something took hold of her chest and squeezed so hard she could not breath. Could that be—? Surely not. The closer they came, though, the more familiar the slung shape looked. A dozen kord out, she could see color and she was sure. When Ia'hi's feet hit stone, Chemel was the first there to unwind the hobble strap from the thin blue wrists of their burden.

"Jiahano!"

She had never been so happy to see anyone in her life. She tore at the hobble on his ankles and helped him to his feet. "Where did they find you? Are you all right?" Two new scars striped the right side of his face from scalp scales to jaw. He carried his right arm stiffly. "What happened after the sled went down? Where are the others?"

Jiahano's nose wrinkled at the sweet reek from her hands. He put his left hand on her shoulder. "Slowly, *mua*. The universe allots us sufficient time to answer questions one at a time."

"I saw him by the *l'i'nean* wall of the Two Springs mesa. I sky-signed for Ia'hi to come help me capture him," Hir'a announced.

Jiahano sighed. "I escaped three days ago from the Shree holding me. I was attempting to reach the observation post."

Chemel was suddenly less delighted to see him. She swore.

Jiahano shrugged. "Perhaps the universe will also give us time for another escape."

G'han danced in excitement. He chattered at Ia'hi, all clicks and whistles. Chemel understood: "Emres . . . *ga'aeree* . . . blades."

Iahi's answer was too fast for Chemel to follow at all but from G'han's scowl, Chemel guessed it was negative.

G'han turned on Jiahano. "What be in your pouches?"

Other Shree eyes brightened in interest. Jiahano looked back steadily, then with slow deliberation emptied the pockets of his jumpsuit. He had very little: the knife from a survival pack's tool kit, the compass and sparker, the needler, also several vials from the drug kit. Last, there was Chemel's map.

Everything was passed around the circle to be handled. Little interested the band except the knife and sparker. Those several adults fingered covetously.

"Choose," Ia'hi said.

G'han snatched the knife.

"You have a good blade," Ra'ab protested. "Mine broke two hunts ago."

Hir'a and Ia'hi exchanged looks. Hir'a removed the knife from G'han's hands and gave it to Ra'ab, ignoring G'han's scowl and flattened ears.

Ala'ka grabbed the sparker. No one disputed her right to it. Hir'a claimed the needler and the drugs from under G'han's reaching hand. "I be an elder. I take them to keep them from young and unwise hands." S's'lis asked for the compass.

That left G'han with the map. He bared his teeth as he picked it up. "Poor *t'k't*."

"You have first choice another time."

G'han unfolded the map. He looked at it, turning it first one way, then the other. As he refolded it, his eyes slid to Chemel and Jiahano. His lips bared another fraction of teeth, then he wheeled, wings clamped tight against his back, and stalked off to his portion of the cave.

"*Ga'aeree*, we be cooking," Me'a'na called.

Chemel grimaced.

Jiahano smiled. "We will talk later, *mua*."

Later was not to be during the meal. Hir'a, Ia'hi, and Asegah dominated that time asking questions directed at Jiahano. They asked the usual ones—what was his world like, where was it, what were his people like? In addition Ia'hi had retrieved the protein analyzer from Chemel's survival pack.

He held it out to Jiahano. "What be this?"

Jiahano regarded it for several minutes, then shook his shoulders in imitation of the negative Shree gesture. "I could not explain it in any way that its function would be comprehensible to you."

Ia'hi flattened his ears. "I think you do not wish to answer."

"I am not permitted to answer."

"Why not?"

G'han rose to his feet with a hiss. "Why do we talk to them? We be the People. We live in the sky. They be only *ga'aeree*, the Wingless Ones, Those Who Walk and Crawl." He stepped over the pots toward Jiahano, spitting the words. He swiped a hand at Jiahano's face, fingers curved like claws. "We do not need to ask *anything* of *ga'aeree*!"

Chemel gasped but Jiahano did not flinch.

"Trade them to the emres for blades and metal!"

Ia'hi's teeth bared. "I have said we cannot. Shishi'ka wishes the *ga'aeree* kept hidden."

"*Shishi'ka* wishes." G'han spat. "What be Shishi'ka? Who has seen him?"

"I have," Hir'a said.

In the sudden silence, G'han's eyes widened. All eyes turned on the aging hunter.

"He came to our band and spoke to our elders in my youth. He be real. He remembers when the great flame-wood trees of the Touch-the-Sky Mountains be no bigger around than my wrist. He told us of the first People and how they drove the first *ga'aeree* from Ne'en with poisoned daggerthorns."

G'han muttered something unintelligible.

"Be silent," Hir'a snapped.

G'han returned to his place and squatted down. He did not say another word for the rest of the meal, only glared at Jiahano and Chemel.

The others in the band were fascinated by Jiahano. They touched him, running fingers over his smooth skin. He bent his head so they could touch the scales on his scalp. He even answered questions, if they were personal ones. Chemel was not astonished at how personal the questions grew once the Shree found what he would answer, but she was astonished at how explicit his answers were, without any signs of embarrassment. She learned more about Mianai biology that evening than she had ever known before.

After the meal Jiahano asked for click sticks. He began with a simple rhythm but before long the percussive pattern grew more and more complex, until the Shree were almost drowning him out with whistles of approval. He challenged and beat both Hib'aki and S's'lis. The band listened hypnotized, no longer interested in either staring or asking questions.

When Jiahano tired of the click sticks, Ia'hi said, "Tell us a story."

Jiahano considered. "If you wish."

Chemel frowned, shaking her head.

He ignored her and began talking. She relaxed. The story was one she had heard in many versions throughout the Sodality, but Jiahano adapted it to Ne'en. He made the story of a wanderer Shree named H'ragar, who flew west to the ocean and brought back the sound of the sea in a shell.

Ia'hi seemed disappointed. Chemel smiled. Had he thought he would trick something else out of Jiahano? The rest of the band, however, loved the story. As soon as Jiahano was finished, they were all eager to tell their favorite stories. Ch'ae finally managed to tell his tale of H'nem and her pet wild Shree, to the shocked delight of the adults, who listened with rapt attention while they covered the ears of the youngsters.

Jiahano moved to the outer edge of the circle and motioned Chemel to slide over beside him.

"You get along well with them," she said.

"My own family has a similar communal structure. There were thirty individuals, adults and children, and no closed doors between any of us, neither psychological nor material."

She stared. She had always imagined Mianai acted with each other as they did with members of other races, each shut away in his own remote tower. "Why—" she began.

He shrugged. "Why do we stand apart? Except for

the Azcarn, your viewpoints are too different. You act and think so fast, tripping over your own minds." He paused. "I feel I am talking like you myself, now, but . . . I cannot describe how lonely these past twenty-odd days have been. One tires of children eventually, no matter how bright or entertaining."

"And it's nice to talk to someone who isn't always asking questions."

He smiled.

She leaned against him. "I do have a couple of questions, though." She kept her voice low, hoping their conversation would attract no attention. "What happened when the sled went down?"

He kept his voice low, too. "We struck the slope near the cliff. I encouraged the others to jump as we rolled, taking their packs with them. On the last roll, I abandoned the sled, too. We were exceedingly lucky and suffered only minor injuries. I had these." He raised his right arm stiffly to touch the scars on his face. "Sheth fractured an arm. Akaara sustained a concussion, I believe. Beyond that we had only abrasions and bruises, and a bloody nose. That was Baezar, I think.

"We lay still on the slope while the illegals' scooter came down to check. They could detect us with an IR scan, obviously, so our only hope was not to move, to appear dead. They soon left. I had brought your map from the pilot compartment so we set a course for the observation post."

"I want to thank you for leaving me the directional marker."

"That was Salah's idea."

Chemel blinked. "Salah?"

"Her words, as nearly as I can recall, were: *'I'm descended from Virinians and I understand them a little. We're her responsibility. She'll be coming after us. Only death will prevent her from coming after us.'* "

Salah had said that? "What happened in the valley?"

"We camped when we thought we were a safe distance from the sled. The next morning, however, we woke to find the sky full of Shree—D'aka'reen, I later found out. Evidently Shishi'ka told them—"

"To capture you. I know that part. And then?"

"They captured us, without much trouble. We were too weak to resist. They were apparently from a number of bands. They divided us among them. My captors traded me for some knife blades a few days later to a T'ka'reen band south of here. I believe those two—" he pointed at S's'lis and Ch'ae—"were with that band at the time."

"Do you know where any of the others are?"

He shook his head. "Have you been planning an escape?"

She dropped her voice still more. "Yes. The chance will come soon. I'll tell you more when we have some privacy." She noticed Ia'hi beginning to eye them. "That was brave of you not to flinch away from G'han."

"I was not brave. He had no intention of touching me. Have you not noticed that for all the flapping of wings and baring of teeth, they never actually strike one another?"

Chemel had not noticed but, thinking back, she could see that that was true.

"Ritualized aggression is not uncommon, *mua*. It is believed that is why the Ilagasans have never had a war—all anger is show."

What she did notice was Ia'hi watching them intently. His ears flicked in their direction, obviously straining to catch every word. He no doubt hoped to overhear bits of information about their worlds and the Sodality.

It was then, watching him and listening to Jiahano, that she thought of a way to find the rest of the team. Make it worth his trouble, and Ia'hi would do it for her.

"It's just as well we were all separated," she said, raising her voice to relieve Ia'hi's earstrain.

Jiahano blinked at her in slow astonishment.

She winked at him with the eye Ia'hi could not see. "It's easy to resist the question they ask when we're alone, but if the whole group of us were to be together, we'd be bound to start talking among ourselves and might discuss some forbidden subjects."

Ia'hi's ears stiffened.

Jiahano lifted his chin in the Shree positive gesture. "That is true. Let there be no more talk tonight, then. Where do we sleep?"

When everyone else headed for their sleeping hides, Chemel took Jiahano to hers. "If we sleep here together, we can talk."

They lay down. With her mouth near his ear, she began whispering of her thunderfoot rope and Hib'aki's impending labor.

"You be going to mate?" a young Shree voice asked.

She looked up. A group of young ones, Ni'in foremost among them, crowded around the column at Jiahano's back, peering down at the *ga'aeree*.

"No, we aren't."

They sighed in disappointment. "I want to see *ga'aeree* mate," Ni'in said.

"Well, we won't do it for you."

Presently their small feet padded away. Chemel sighed in exasperation. In Jiahano's chest, though, she felt the vibration of a silent chuckle. It was infectious; her sigh turned to a giggle.

Despite her lack of sexual desire for the Mianai, she still found his nearness enormously satisfying. What a pleasant herbal odor his skin had. Jiahano was not the only one who had been lonely, she realized. Snuggling closer, she drifted off to sleep with a last fervent wish willing Ia'hi to take the bait they had laid.

Chapter Nine

Ia'hi was watching them again. Everytime Chemel and Jiahano had come near each other during the past three days, the Shree managed to be nearby, eyes watchful, ears cocked toward them.

Chemel paused while grinding grain to raise a brow at Jiahano. "Is he thinking, do you suppose?"

Jiahano nodded as he poured a little more grain into her mortar.

"Let's feed him more bait."

"One wonders," Jiahano said in measured syllables, "whether these are true primitives progressing toward higher civilization or sophisticates retreating from complex society. The Woon of Piloo have been offered every possible aid to help them regain their former level of civilization, all of which they refuse. After studying them for thirty-five years, my conclusion was that after the initial collapse of their society, the vandals who robbed the crops every harvest discouraged them from attempting to maintain even an agricultural level. They retreated to the hunter/gatherer society, where no one possesses more than he must for survival, nothing worth stealing."

Ia'hi edged closer, pretending to be interested in something in the sky outside.

Jiahano looked up, starting, as if seeing Ia'hi for the first time. He stopped talking.

Ia'hi sighed in obvious disappointment. He turned his back to the edge of the entrance. Stretching out his wings, he began scratching his back against the rock. "Who be the Woon of Piloo?"

Chemel pretended to frown in disapproval at Jiahano. "No one."

Ia'hi leaned harder against the stone, working his upper shoulder. "I be thinking."

Chemel drew a slow breath and leaned into the grinding stone. Push . . . pull . . . push.

"You be happy to see this other *ga'aeree*."

She nodded, then corrected the gesture to a double lift of her chin.

"It would make you happy to see other *ga'aeree*?"

"Yes." She said it without emotion and did not pause grinding. Her heart galloped, however.

"I will find the others for you. How many be there?"

"Five." Now she stopped grinding to look up at him. "One is black like the rock towers. One is yellow and looks like a lizard, a *hir'a*. One is like me but . . . fatter. One is smaller than me with hair and eyes the color of She'shee's coat. The last is dun-colored and looks like some of the hoofed animals. He has four legs and two arms."

"I can find them by visiting all the bands I know." He frowned. "It might upset *t'k't*."

Chemel bit her lip, but said nothing. She resumed grinding. She could not help him talk himself into this.

"I do not know how to make the other bands give us their *ga'aeree*."

The band that captured Jiahano had traded him. That seemed an obvious answer. The temptation to tell him was almost overwhelming. How much harm could one little piece of advice cause, especially if it helped her recover the team? She sighed, thinking of what her father had always said about rules. When they existed, they were to be followed, no matter how personally inconvenient. *Anything* she might offer would be interference.

She bent her head over the grinding stone. Push . . . pull . . . push. "You're very clever, Ia'hi. You can find a way."

On the edge of her vision she saw him stand away from the stone. He folded his wings, watching her, then he turned and walked back into the cave.

Well, she had done the "right" thing. Was it right? For once, she could not be sure.

Jiahano's languid voice came from behind her. "I am struck by the possibility that in not offering him a solution, you may have done more than you would by speaking."

She looked up.

"You are forcing him into mental activity, stimulating intellectual processes that might otherwise have remained inactive."

Her heart dropped. She sat back on her calves. "You mean it's possible I'm interfering no matter *what* I do?" she asked in dismay.

"In a sense."

"Thank you." Bitterly, she picked up the mortar and dumped the flour into a storage jar. She slapped the mortar back down. "More grain." Damned if she did, and damned if she did not. They had to leave. It was the only possible solution. She wished Hib'aki would start labor.

Jiahano touched her shoulder. "It is only speculation."

"Maybe, but it has a valid ring to it."

She ground until the jar was full of flour, then carried the jar back to the cooking area. She saw Ia'hi squatting nearby, watching a group of young Shree stretch the skin of an *ibee,* a lion mouse, in a miniature curing frame. He scratched an ear in thought.

Through the rest of the day she saw him watching various members of the band, examining everything they did. He picked up the harness Asegah was finishing and put it down with a shake of his shoulders. Later she saw him with She'shee's portrait of her, then with some of Ch'ni's red bowls. He put down the bowls when a quarrel broke out on the far side of the cave.

Everyone headed for the noise.

G'han and Ra'ab faced each other across two kord of space. They held their wings stiffly extended and snarled at each other, the full length of their teeth exposed.

Chemel pieced together the conversation from the Shree words she knew.

"I offer you a fair trade," G'han growled. "Give me the *ga'aeree* blade."

Ra'ab shook his lower shoulders. "No trade. You offer me nothing I wish more than the blade."

G'han snatched up a small clay bowl from a shelf behind him and hurled it at Ra'ab. It missed him by a good third of a kord, but it struck a column behind him. As the bowl shattered, shards exploded outward in all directions. One caught Ra'ab in the back of the head.

Ra'ab shrieked as if mortally wounded. He bent over, clutching at his head.

In the general rush to touch and comfort the howling Shree, G'han reached him first and fussed most over the tiny drop of blood that stained the sandy-red coat.

Only Ia'hi did not join the group around Ra'ab. He ran a finger down Chemel's arm. "Come."

Chemel and Jiahano followed him to one of the cave entrances. There he squatted down and motioned for them to join him. Chemel sat down cross-legged.

Ia'hi regarded her with steady eyes. "We will trade for the other *ga'aeree.* We must find something the

People who hold the others will want more than the *ga'aeree*."

He wanted her suggestions? Fortunately she had none. "They're your people. You know their needs best."

"Metal," he said promptly. "Metal for flashers and blades and pots. Ch'ni's bowls, perhaps, as well."

She could not help questioning that. "Why the red bowls? Hasn't Shishi'ka taught everyone to make them?"

He blinked. "Shishi'ka did not teach Ch'ni. She learned alone."

Ch'ni had refined the bowl design and discovered that beautiful glaze by herself? It seemed incredible, but Chemel was more willing to believe that now than she would have twenty-six days ago.

Ia'hi stared past her out the entrance. "We need metal."

Chemel sat silently, waiting for him to go on. When he did not, she asked, "Where do you get metal?"

"Some the emres give us. The mountain bands know how to take metal from rock, also."

Chemel remembered that Me'a'na's metal pot came from the mountains.

"We must trade with the mountain bands for metal," Ia'hi said.

What did they trade? The mountains were rich in all resources. Chemel rubbed a brow tuft.

"What do the mountain bands want more than metal?" Ia'hi asked.

Chemel tucked in her chin. She saw Jiahano look away, fingers across his lips like a set of bars. Did he know?

Ia'hi sighed. He scratched his ears and frowned. He brushed unseen dust from the membrane of the wing-tips curling forward between his legs. He chewed on his fingernails.

Chemel hugged her knees and waited in silence, watching him struggle through the process of thinking.

She was interfering by doing nothing, but what else could she do?

The sun sank toward the horizon. Chemel watched it, measuring it from time to time with the width of her hand. One handspan . . . two.

Finally Ia'hi put hands on his knees and pushed up to his feet. He looked west. "I will ask."

He left the next morning. The pouches of his harness bulged with an assortment of portable samples. His departure aroused feverish curiosity in the rest of the band and indignation that he had not confided the reason for his sudden urge to travel.

They began to speculate why he left. It became a running game they took up at odd moments between hunts and chores over the next few days, with each suggestion more outrageous and slanderous than the last. At any one time, the game lasted until everyone was doubled over, wheezing in laughter. Even Chemel and Jiahano laughed along with the others.

Only Hib'aki was not amused. Her temper shortened with each round until, on the sixth day, she picked up a bowl of *t'a'zah* and began throwing the roots. Everyone ducked, even though Hib'aki did not come within a kord of hitting anyone, and they fell over laughing at her acid opinions on the number of *z'z'ras* in their immediate ancestry.

"Why is she so upset?" Chemel asked.

Even from below Chemel's shoulder, Ala'ka managed to look down her nose. "Ia'hi sires her young ones."

How did they know? She understood that actual mating occurred only in winter, when the females came into estrus, but she saw and heard plenty of indiscriminate noncoital sex play at night and on idle days. Were the pairings stricter in actual mating? Interpersonal relationships were one aspect of Shree life still incomprehensible to her.

Chemel returned to her mortar and grinding stone. At least she understood those. Today she was helping

Ch'ni prepare clay for potmaking by grinding dried lumps of clay into powder.

Chemel sighed while she pounded. "Grind grain, grind *ch'ee'a'bae*, grind clay. Jiahano, I'm going to have shoulders a kord wide by the time we leave here."

Jiahano turned from picking up the roots Hib'aki had thrown. He smiled. "If you should happen to resign from DSC, at least you will have a skill on which to—" He broke off, head snapping up. "Stop pounding."

Chemel stopped. "What is it?"

"What do you hear?"

She listened. She heard the young ones play a noisy game across the cave and Ch'ae entreating She'shee to come flying with him. She heard the wind outside. She heard—she heard a distant hum, a sound almost below the threshold of perception.

"Grid drive!"

Jiahano grabbed her wrist. Pulling her to her feet, he headed for the rear of the cave moving faster than she had ever seen him move. He kept hold of her wrist, but she kept the pace without the need for him to pull her.

They paused at the mouth of one of the tunnels that had not been cross-tunneled like the fore part of the cave. There were no lamps there and they should be impossible for anyone near the front to see.

A shadow crossed the cave entrance.

"Scooter." Her pulse throbbed in her throat and ears.

The hum stopped. A few moments later the sound of wings reached them . . . but not membrane wings. Chemel pulled farther back into the dark of the tunnel.

Another shadow crossed the entrance. A silhouette of feathered wings projected into the sunlight on the cave floor. The shadow wings closed and the living being stepped onto the rock. The Aranen stood dark against the brightness outside, but Chemel still saw the blue aerie markings on the gold wings.

"*Ha t'k't*," Thiil called.

The members of the band converged on the visitor. They all spoke Pan, but the overlay of voices made understanding them impossible.

Only Thiil's lisping accent stood by itself. "I've come looking for *ga'aeree*. Their craft fell in one of your valleys a short flight south of here. They escaped alive but now they're lost. I'm trying to find them."

G'han said, "We have seen sky signing about such. The sky signs say you be offering metal to the People for *ga'aeree*?"

Chemel clenched her fists. Damn that little savage! She wished him an instant and fiery destruction.

"That's true. I'm offering *ga'aeree* blades, and metal for decoration and pots."

"I—" G'han began on a note of eagerness, only to break off in a shriek. Chemel hoped he were *really* hurt.

Hir'a's voice rose over G'han's. "I be interested in metal."

Chemel swore under her breath in impotent rage. Hir'a, too?

"I wish we knew where *ga'aeree* be," Hir'a went on.

Chemel blessed him silently, leaning back against the rock in relief.

"We have seen no *ga'aeree*." Hir'a dripped regret from every syllable.

"None?" Thiil's beak snapped. "They were going northeast. They would have to have spent some time in your territory."

The band sighed collectively. "No *ga'aeree*."

"But I see one of their packs over against that column." The tone in Thiil's voice was suspicious and stubborn.

Chemel's heart plunged again. She had forgotten about the pack.

"Yes," Hir'a said without hesitation. "We found that by the broken machine. "There be two hands of them."

Chemel pictured him holding up the fingers and thumb

of one hand and the three fingers of the other. "They be divided to keep *t'k't*."

"Too bad you found just the packs. Well, I haven't come just looking for *ga'aeree*. I like to visit my friends among the People. I've brought gifts. Let's sit down and talk."

They all squatted down. Chemel slid down the glassy fused rock of the tunnel wall to the floor. "Make yourself comfortable, Jiahano. We may be here for a while."

Although Chemel later decided it was no more than an hour or so, *a while* became eternity when she had to spend it pressed against the hard rock of the tunnel, her buttocks going numb while she strained to hear what was being said up front.

Jiahano's hearing was sharper than hers. "It has the sound of mere chatter," he told her, "but under it all our hosts are sounding Thiil for information on outside worlds and, simultaneously, Thiil is posing questions whose answers must indicate a familiarity with the appearance and habits of our group."

To her relief, neither succeeded. The comments Jiahano reported Thiil gave were verbose without containing much information. The band's replies to his probes were equally obscure. G'han had very little to say.

When Thiil finally made his farewells and the scooter lifted off, she and Jiahano staggered out of hiding. G'han glared at them with smoldering eyes, but not at them alone. The rest of the band came in for its share of glares, too.

They paid little attention, however. They were too busy strutting around Chemel and Jiahano.

"He be trying to trick us into talking of you," Hir'a said.

"It sounded like that, yes."

"He could not trick us. We be too clever."

"We should have traded them."

Hir'a laid back his ears. "*Sh'sha*, G'han."

"I wish to have a *ga'aeree* blade."

"You don't like *ga'aeree* but you certainly covet what we can give you, don't you?" Chemel said.

That earned her a silent snarl. G'han stalked to the entrance and threw himself into the air.

The band looked after him, looked at each other, tucked in their chins, and went back to what they had been doing before Thiil arrived.

Chemel resumed grinding Ch'ni's clay. She found her fingers shaky on the grinding stone. "G'han makes me nervous, Jiahano. How long can Shishi'ka's wishes override greed?"

Jiahano squatted next to her and lowered his voice. "Are you thinking, then, that we should leave as soon as the opportunity offers itself?"

"I'm thinking that, yes."

"And what of the chance to find the others?"

She dumped the clay powder into a large bowl Ch'ni had given her and added enough water to soak the powder, then put more lumps into the mortar. "Do you think we can find them before G'han goes to Thiil?"

He tucked in his chin.

She raised a brow tuft at the gesture. "Do you think we can do it before we go hopelessly native?"

He blinked, then his mouth stretched into a slow smile. "You are learning to joke, *mua*."

They broke off the conversation to move aside for exiting hunters. As usual, the decision to hunt or not to hunt seemed to have been made on impulse. The hunters picked up their spears and dove out the entrance laughing and joking.

Chemel stared after them. "I always thought of primitives as struggling day to day for survival, but the Shree never seem to worry about going hungry."

"The hunter/gatherer life need not be a difficult one. It is the agricultural and industrial societies that must work every day."

Ni'in looked wistfully after the hunters. "I will go with them soon."

Chemel glanced toward him. For once, he was not carrying his *m'im*. Instead, he wore a harness, a miniature of the adults'. He thrust out his chest to show it off. "I be learning to fly."

"Not today," Ibee said from back in the cave.

His eyes pleaded. "*Amma?*"

"No. Come to me."

He went, sighing.

Chemel, who could understand most of what Ibee said, heard the Shree continue. "First you must practice wing strokes. Later I will take you into the air with this." She held up a long line of braided hide. "Then if you weaken, I have this and you cannot fall."

Chemel eyed the tether. Now, that was a way the Shree could transport nonflyers in more comfort than the hobbles. She was fascinated by the idea of a Shree having to learn to fly. She had thought it was instinctive. Perhaps it was like climbing. Children climbed rocks and trees, but doing it skillfully and safely so that one could scale mountains took instruction and practice.

In late afternoon she and Jiahano were carrying Ch'ni's bowl, heavy with the clay-and-water slurry, back into the cave when one of the young ones called, "The hunters be back. Ia'hi be with them!"

Chemel raced for the entrance with everyone else.

They came down in a thunderous thrum of wings, carrying two fly goats. Ia'hi touched rock last. Head and shoulders above the Shree, Chemel thought she was in a good position to catch his eye, but she could not. Ia'hi was fully occupied with his own people. Even the necessity of stringing up the two carcasses and skinning them out did not hamper their questions. Straining to catch his answers, Chemel thought he told them only that he had been to the mountains for a reason he would tell them later.

That did not help her. Had he learned what he needed to? She tried to read his expression, to find satisfaction or even disappointment in it. To her frustration, she could detect neither.

She tried speaking to him. "Ia'hi."

He looked at her, then, but immediately turned away to say something to Hir'a.

She hissed through her teeth.

"Patience, *mua*," Jiahano said.

"You mean, wait until *he's* ready to talk to *me*?" She sighed.

She waited through preparation of the meal, and through eating it. She was not the only one waiting, but the rest of the band were not interested in patience. They kept asking, obliquely and directly, what he was going to tell them. Ia'hi ignored them as easily as he ignored Chemel.

The only members of the band he talked to were Hir'a and Asegah. After the meal the three of them moved off to one side in a tight little group. They spoke in voices too low to be heard by anyone else. Whenever the rest of the band tried to edge within hearing range, Asegah exercised his authority as an elder and sent them back with a flick of a finger.

Chemel and Jiahano sat down in one of the entrances. With sunset, the sky had cleared. The air still smelled of dust but its color had become clear cobalt. Somewhere down the valley, a pinna fox sang: "*Hie-ie-ie.*"

Jiahano answered in a very good imitation of the fox's cry. The fox sang back.

Jiahano looks at peace, Chemel thought enviously. She wished she felt that way. Instead, she kept looking back over her shoulder at the group of three Shree, wondering when Ia'hi was going to speak to her . . . wondering *if* he were going to speak to her at all. He might not feel any need to tell a mere *ga'aeree* what he had learned in the mountains.

As the evening deepened, the members of the band lighted the lamps in the cave. The voice of the pinna fox faded into nighttime silence.

When Chemel was numb from sitting on the rock, Ia'hi finally stood up and came over to her. "The mountain clans will trade for the secret of Ch'ni's pottery and for *mi'inae'mi*."

"What's that?"

He took two pieces of blue stone from a pouch on his harness and dropped them in her hand. She recognized them as a copper and aluminum phosphate mineral called *skyeye* throughout most of the Sodality. Great deposits of it lay all over Virini. On her world, however, the opaque gemstone occurred mostly in a pure blue form. In this piece a fine network of green veins marbled the blue.

"You can find this easily?"

He lifted his chin, then took back the sample stones and walked away.

Chemel met Jiahano's eyes. "They'll take skyeye for metal." There was still a chance to bring the team together again . . . a chance. She took the thought to bed with her and fell asleep thinking about it.

A cry woke her. Chemel sat up, fighting for orientation. Around her, feet shuffled on stone. Sparks jumped from flints as lamps were lighted.

She touched Jiahano. "What is it?"

He pointed toward adult and young Shree converging on Hib'aki's sleeping area.

She understood. "Hib'aki's started labor."

Hib'aki groaned. The band crowded around her, murmuring.

Chemel hugged her knees to her chest. It was just as she thought it would be; all attention was focused on Hib'aki. She knew the location of every piece of equipment she wanted. Using Asegah's rope, they could rappel down the cliff. It would be a safe descent even in the dark. They could be gone for hours before anyone noticed they were missing.

Yet . . . the mountain bands would trade skyeye for metal, and metal might buy the team from the bands that held them. Or it might not, and G'han might decide to sell them all to Thiil.

She felt Jiahano's eyes on her. "What do you think?" she whispered. "Should we leave or not?"

He tucked in his chin. "I am not qualified to offer a fair opinion. I am an anthropologist, after all, not a monitor. I leave it to your judgment."

Her judgment? She leaned her forehead against her updrawn knees. When they first landed, she wanted them to look to her for decisions. Now . . .

Leaving was removing their interference from the Shree. Leaving was safer, considering the danger G'han posed. Leaving was following the rules. Staying gave her a chance to meet her responsibilities to the team. Which duty was more important?

She heard Hib'aki groaning, more sharply now, and the Shree chattering around her. Some joked. Others offered encouragement. The young Shree clicked and whistled excitedly.

"We must decide soon, *mua.*" Jiahano's voice came softly, but insistently.

She could rationalize that to leave the team scattered would risk an incalculable amount of interference whereas the miners posed a lesser danger, being less intimately associated with the natives. She was not sure, though. What, she wondered, had happened to her clear sense of knowing what was best?

"I want to get the team together again. I'm responsible for them. I have to find out what's happened to them and if they're all right. We'll stay and risk what G'han might do."

Only then did she lift her head and look at Jiahano. She realized she hoped to see from his reaction whether he approved of her decision or not. His smooth face revealed nothing, however. She put her head down again, and hoped she had chosen wisely.

Chapter Ten

Hib'aki did not look like someone who had ended the night screaming as if being butchered. She sang and murmured and hummed while she laid her newborn son on an *afa'haf*—tiger-wolf—pelt in the midday sun at the entrance of the cave. She held her wings entended as a barrier to hold everyone back, adults, young ones, and curious *m'im* alike.

The newest member of the band, a creature so tiny Chemel thought she could easily hold him in one open hand, blinked unfocused cobalt eyes at the world. Silky white fur covered him, and his ears lay flat against his head while his wings balled like tiny pink fists. Chemel longed to pick him up, or even just to touch him. She did not beg to do so, though, unlike everyone else.

Instead, she looked over at Ia'hi. He did not appear to be someone who had spent the night comforting his mate. He paid no attention at all to his offspring. Instead, he paced behind the band, snapping his wings open and closed and hissing through his teeth in a frustrated attempt to attract some attention.

"I be going to the emres for *mi'inae'mi*. Who will help me bring it back?"

Chemel lost all interest in the infant. "I'll come," she said in Pan.

His upper lip pulled back from his teeth. "You have grown wings, perhaps?" Then he stared. "You understand the People's tongue?" He said that in his own language.

She swore at herself. She should never have responded to him. Outwardly, she gave him a blank, uncomprehending stare and hoped he would think her comment was a coincidence.

He met her stare with a suspicious one of his own, but broke it to look at Hir'a when the aging hunter said, "I will help you."

Bi'nrar and G'han turned around. "You be going where?"

Ia'hi explained, and told them why he wanted the gemstones. Both Shree frowned.

Bi'nrar's ears twitched. "All the *ga'aeree* here? That will upset *t'k't*."

Ia'hi shook his lower shoulders. "Trading keeps *t'k't*."

"I wish no more *ga'aeree* here," G'han said.

She'shee turned around. "I will come, too."

That meant S's'lis and Ch'ae also volunteered, bringing the party to seven.

"Let us trade with the mountains clans for metal but keep the metal," G'han said.

If he expected the suggestion to be welcomed, he was disappointed. Ia'hi snarled and laid back his ears. "No!"

"Then I will not come."

They tucked in their chins and walked away.

Chemel hurried after them. "Take me along, too."

She said it in Pan. Ia'hi answered likewise. "It be too difficult."

"It isn't. I can wear a harness. Attach two tethers to

it like the ones used for training flights, and you hold those."

Ia'hi's ears twitched. He chewed a fingernail. "Why do you wish to go? To escape?"

"To the emres?" She shook her shoulders. "They'd kill me. I just want to see what the emres are like."

"Kill?" Hir'a frowned dubiously.

She did not care to try explaining murder to these people. Hastily, she said, "I used an incorrect word. I want to go to see the emres. I won't show myself to them and I won't try to escape."

Ia'hi and Hir'a exchanged doubtful glances.

She bit her lip. She needed to see just what the miners were doing, and she longed to get out of the cave. "Take me. *Amma?*"

Perhaps it was her use of the word the young ones used to beg favors from adults. Ia'hi and Hir'a considered several minutes longer, whispering together, then they lifted their chins in assent. "Find a harness that will fit you."

She turned to find Jiahano regarding her with his scalp furrowed in concern. "Do you realize what you just did?"

"I gave them a suggestion." She sighed. "I know it's wrong, but . . . I have to go with them, and since it's of no benefit to them if I do, I can't force them into thinking of an easy method of transporting me."

"What is it you hope to learn?"

"I don't know." She smiled wryly. "Anything will be more than I know now. Please, help me find a harness I can wear."

An old one belonging to Ia'hi was the largest they could find. Even let out to its longest length it was small. The straps cut deep into Chemel's neck and buttocks. Airborne in it some half-hour later, holding on to the tether lines stretching up to Ia'hi and Bi'nrar flying wingtip to wingtip above her, she reflected it was fortunate she was thin. If she had been plump like

Salah, no matter how strong her desire to do so, she could never have squeezed into the harness.

After that she forgot any discomfort in the pleasure of the moment. Now she could see around her as they flew. The air slid coldly around her face, feet, and hands, and beneath her shirt and trousers to her body. She welcomed the chill. She felt comfortable for the first time since her capture. Now she knew why Kiris had said just seeing through the eyes of a flying creature without feeling the air was not flying at all. What did it feel like to pull up into the sky on one's own wings? She tried to imagine the sensation.

The flight lay west and lasted about two hours, putting them deep in D'aka'reen territory. Those in the party did not act as if they considered themselves invaders, though. They passed D'aka'reen Shree in the sky, and the exchanged greetings all appeared friendly. The territorial bounds were not jealously guarded, then, Chemel concluded.

They came down in a valley not much different from the one below the Sun Cliff cave. Ia'hi untied the tether from his harness. Bi'nrar, however, kept his line attached. He took Chemel by the arm and pulled her into a small grove of plate-leaf trees. "We will see from here."

See what? she wondered. Where were the miners? She repeated the questions aloud.

Bi'nrar pointed. "Watch the others."

Hir'a led the group. He climbed the slope, sending a small band of fly goats scrambling away. A cliff cat, her stalk spoiled, leaped from behind a rock and chased the band. Fly goats and cliff cat alike climbed straight up the cliff face, picking their way through the blooming red riser vines that shrouded the rock. Birds nesting behind the vines exploded out of the path of the chase; the sharp whirs of their wings carried clearly down to where Chemel waited, wondering where the Shree could be heading. Not until they were almost at the cliff face did she see that the slope in a small area had been leveled. What she had at first taken to be an indentation in the cliff she realized now was a doorway. An air sled with a hopper replacing the usual cargo compartment rolled out through the door and lifted off.

Chemel watched the sled rise. So they worked completely underground and took the rock they dug out to some other point. The tailings were no doubt distributed so as to be unnoticeable from the air. Emre still had the problem of shipping back to the Sodality, however, and accounting for the cargo. How did they accomplish that?

The Shree reached the opening and stepped through.

Chemel rubbed a brow tuft. "How will they get the *mi'inae'mi* from the emres?"

"Ask for it. Emres must give us some of what they dig when we ask, to keep *t'k't*."

Chemel snorted at the idea of an illegal miner caring whether he kept the universe in balance. "What would you do if they started refusing to share with you?"

Bi'nrar considered, scratching an ear. "Shishi'ka has taught us that the emres promised to keep *t'k't* when our foremothers let them begin digging. If they do not keep *t'k't*, Ka will come to adjust."

She sighed. How naively trusting they were.

"Or," Bi'nrar continued in the same tone, "we can put sweetvine juice on our speartips and drive the emres fron Ne'en as our foremothers did the first *ga'aeree*."

"How are they going to ask the emres for the stone? I thought the emres won't talk to you."

"Some do. The others do not . . . like that one."

He looked past her. Chemel whirled. A figure was approaching the plate-leaf trees . . . a Mianai. Chemel looked around quickly for somewhere to hide. Would ducking around to the other side of the tree work?

"Good afternoon."

It was too late to hide now. She turned to face him. "Good afternoon. It's . . . warm, isn't it?"

He looked her down with the same aloof amusement

that used to annoy her in Jiahano. "By Virinian standards, perhaps. Are you a member of a local crew? I do not recall having seen you before."

"I'm . . . new. My name is . . . Athe Vren."

"I am Nokahole Debaeliname, geologist."

Mianai names could be set to music, Chemel mused.

"You are a hunter, perhaps?" he asked.

She blinked, then said, "Yes. How did you know?"

He eyed her clothes and bare feet. "They often exhibit a tendency to atavism."

He looked at and talked to her, but not once had his eyes focused on Bi'nrar. Why not? "My companion is a hunter, too."

The geologist looked around. "Companion?"

Beside her, Bi'nrar said, "They do not see us. See?" He pulled his upper lip back in a snarl. He danced in place with hands drawn into claws, and shrieked piercingly.

The geologist did not even blink. Chemel stared at him. Now could that be possible? Unless . . .

"How many limbs do the local animals have?" she asked.

It took several seconds, but surprise rippled his detachment. "What an extraordinary question. Why do you ask?"

"Curiosity about your answer."

"Very well. The local fauna are quadrupeds, as are the life forms on nearly two-thirds of the worlds habitable to us."

Quadrupeds! That almost proved her suspicion. "What's the name of this planet?"

His forehead furrowed. "You may be new, but I believe the sun is already affecting you adversely. You should wear your hood up. The planet is Tregre, of course. Where else did you think you might be?"

Emre had to be using a mind block on its crews. It was the obvious solution, now that she considered it. They took a charter on Tregre, which was probably somewhere in the local star group, and set up a cover mining operation there. Then they planted a mind block in the crews sent to Ne'en, making the workers think they had gone to Tregre. She imagined that cargoes coming from Ne'en all listed Tregre as their point of origin.

Not all the personnel were mind-blocked, of course. Like Thiil and the Azcarn, supervisors and higher-ups needed to know where they really were in order to handle the necessary dealings with the Shree.

"I won't keep you any longer," she told the geologist.

Smiling faintly, he nodded. "So I am dismissed, Virinian? Thank you. Good afternoon."

She and Bi'nrar watched him walk on down the valley, kicking over rocks as he went, occasionally leaning down to pick up and examine one.

"Why do they not see us?"

Chemel smiled at the Shree's tone of annoyance. "They have a kind of blindness."

"Emres and *ga'aeree* be strange."

Up the slope, at the opening into the mesa, the Shree appeared again. With them was an Aranen. For a moment Chemel's heart jumped, then she saw the aerie markings were green. Still, she kept in the trees, out of sight.

The group stood talking for several minutes, then the Aranen disappeared back inside and the Shree came down toward the trees. The large skin bag each had brought bulged with rock. Chemel's brow tufts rose. The miners had given them *that* much skyeye?

The Shree reached the trees. Ia'hi held out his bag. "Take part of this, Bi'nrar."

They transferred half the contents to the bag Bi'nrar carried. Chemel saw what the miners had given them was raw rock, not just skyeye. The gemstone would have to be broken free before it could be used.

They lashed the sacks to their harnesses. Ia'hi and Bi'nrar juggled rock until they had theirs evenly divided between them, then they lashed on their sacks, too, and Ia'hi tied Chemel's other tether to himself.

"You saw what you wished?" Ia'hi asked her.

She lifted her chin. "I saw what I wanted, *ba.*"

The group sprang into the air. As Ia'hi and Bi'nrar launched together, Chemel grabbed the tethers and set herself for the jerk that lifted her off the ground moments later.

The flight home was uneventful, but slower. They stopped midway to rest. The Shree spent the time not lying down, however, but examining some bushes and poking the ground with a spear Ch'ae had brought.

"The *ala'ki'bae* be blooming," She'shee said, touching the yellow blossoms on the bushes. "There be berries ten or twenty hunts from now."

S's'lis found a patch of brilliant red flowers. Using Ch'ae's spear point, he dug them up. The Shree broke off the bulbous roots and stuffed them into empty pouches on their harnesses.

Chemel wrinkled her nose at the strong, spicy scent suddenly filling the air. So that was where those roots came from.

"Remember the place the berries grow," Hir'a said.

The second leg of the flight was even slower than the first. Chemel wondered if they should have spent the rest time resting instead of checking around for food. It made her wonder, too, how long carrying a load of skyeye would make the flight to the mountain bands. More, how would they manage all that metal they needed to bring back?

After the evening meal, while Chemel was feeding the pot scrapings to the *m'im,* Jiahano came and sat beside her. "You seem preoccupied, *mua.* What did you discover about the miners?"

She told him. She also told him her concern about transporting the trade goods. "I wish we had a sled."

He looked at her. "Not really, I trust."

She considered. "No, not really." Most of her monitor's training was still intact. "Did anything interesting happen here this afternoon?"

"Everyone played with Hib'aki's baby, of course. Ibee gave Ni'in a flying lesson, although he less flew than glided."

"What did G'han do?"

"He squatted against a column and watched me. He is thinking hard. I am not yet certain whether or not to be concerned about those thoughts."

She looked around for G'han and found him near the oven in the cooking area, watching them. "They concern me. Did he leave at any time?"

"Not that I observed."

In the circle of lamps where the meal had been, the sacks of stone were emptied. Ia'hi stood with arms folded, staring at the rock. He pushed one piece around with a foot and murmured to Hir'a. Chemel strained to hear while she helped Ch'ni and Ala'ka scour out the cooking pots with sand.

"What is he saying?" she asked Ala'ka.

"He be saying how tiring the flight be carrying the rock."

So she was not the only one to think about it. She finished cleaning her share of the pots as quickly as possible and moved to join Jiahano where she could hear. By that time most of the adults were squatted down around the skyeye rock regarding it with frowns.

"The *mi'inae'mi* alone will be lighter," Ia'hi said.

Asegah rubbed an ear. "Still too heavy for two or three to carry. We cannot send all our flyers to the mountains. Some must stay to hunt and gather."

Chemel bit her lip. Two or three could never bring back all the metal.

"We can make several trips."

"At six days each trip? That be six days you cannot hunt. How many days must you be gone to trade metal for the *ga'aeree*? You cannot hunt then, either, but we be having more and more to feed, ones who cannot fly and cannot help gather food. What will the *ga'aeree* say to make them worth so much trouble?"

Chemel hugged her knees with a sinking in her stomach.

"They know many things. They have ideas and machines. I wish to understand such things." Ia'hi went to his sleeping area and brought back the protein analyzer and the needler. "Machines like this might be useful to us."

Asegah handled the analyzer and the needler, then returned them. "I be thinking that this be poor *t'k't*. I think we cannot do this."

Ia'hi looked at Hir'a.

Hir'a sighed. "Perhaps the elder speaks a truth."

Chemel's heart dropped. She leaned her forehead against her knees and swore silently, despairingly. She understood the old Shree's arguments; there was *not* much value to the Shree in finding the team, not for as much effort as it would take. They could not allow satisfying curiosity to take precedence over the welfare of the band, and yet ... *damn!*

She lifted her head. "If there were a way to carry on the trade without taking so many hunters away from the band, would you let Ia'hi do it?"

Several pairs of eyes widened but Asegah did not seem surprised to find her responding in Pan to conversation carried on in the Shree language. "I cannot forbid Ia'hi to do this. The People all belong to themselves. I only advise from the wisdom of my age and experience."

Giving advice that younger Shree almost always followed. She tried again. "If there were a way to trade using fewer hunters, would you stop advising against it?"

He considered. "Perhaps. What be the way?"

She sighed. "I don't know yet; I just wanted to see what your response might be if there were."

"When you find a way, ask me again."

She leaned her forehead against her knees. An arm slid around her shoulders and squeezed, then withdrew.

"Be comforted, *mua*. All things pass, even disappointments."

She did not find that thought particularly comforting. Life passed, too. In the meantime, she still had five members of the study team scattered out across the Firestone Territory. She must find them somehow. She was determined to do so.

Mentally, she stood back and stared at herself. Was this Monitor Chemel Krar thinking? Would she look for the team even at the cost of interference? Would she go that far?

"*Ga'aeree.*"

She lifted her head to find Ia'hi standing over her. They were almost alone. The band, Jiahano included, was forming another circle on the far side of the scattered skyeye rock. She heard the first tentative notes of Asegah's flute.

"*Ga'aeree,* the elder speaks a truth."

Suddenly she was annoyed at being addressed by a label. "My name is Chemel."

"I still wish to gather the *ga'aeree*, but I cannot force others to fly with me. You know a way for me to trade alone?"

She did not. She wished she did. "You have a clever mind, Ia'hi. You don't need me to tell you how to do things." She interfered if she helped; she interfered if she did not. Damn. "However, if I think of a way, I'll tell you." The lie made her sound willing to be cooperative.

"While we be thinking, you help take the *mi'inae'mi* from the stone." He pointed at the raw rock.

Wryly, she reflected she might have known she would inherit that job. She flexed her shoulders. They would be two kord wide by the time she left Ne'en.

She spent the next two days with the hammer from the survival pack's tool kit, chipping skyeye pieces free of the stone holding them. Jiahano helped when he could, but there was only one hammer and breaking rock with other rock was difficult as well as tedious. She accomplished the most.

Ia'hi took long flights by himself. Though he brought back furry herbivores, gamebirds, and even some small predators like cliff cats, Chemel suspected that hunting was an automatic activity while his real objective each time was the solitude. In the cave he prowled restlessly, brooding, snarling at everyone. Members of the band began avoiding him.

Ni'in appeared to be the only Shree enjoying the situation. Every time he became too boisterous, Ibee hurried him out for a flying lesson.

Once Hir'a squatted down beside Chemel. "Shishi'ka asks us to keep you or I would help you escape. *Ga'aeree* should not be here. The idea of them has taken Ia'hi out of *t'k't*. You must leave."

Chemel reflected that there is always more than one path between two points. "I can't go without the others."

"Then I must help Ia'hi."

"I will help, too."

Chemel and Hir'a looked around. She'shee stood behind them. "I be tired of S's'lis and Ch'ae. I would like to see the mountains."

That was three. Chemel eyed the growing pile of skyeye. "Three still won't be enough to bring the metal back."

She'shee sniffed. "Two can bring the metal back."

Chemel stared up at the female. "You know a way to do that?"

She'shee lifted her chin. *"Ba."*

"Why didn't you say so before?"

"No one asked me."

Chemel stood, sighing. What people. "I'm asking now. How can two flyers bring back all the metal necessary to trade for *ga'aeree*?"

"The emres have machines where they dig. They

pull them. With them, one emre may take more than he could carry."

"They're called trucks. You mean to pull a truck through the mountains and back?"

She'shee hissed in disgust. "We be not *ga'aeree* who must crawl along the ground! I will put wings on the truck and pull it *over* the mountains . . . like that." She led them to the entrance and pointed into the sky, at Ni'in with wings locked in a glide position being towed behind Ibee on the tether. "It be simple."

Chemel grinned. "You're remarkable."

"I be very clever, too. I should go tell Ia'hi, *ba?*"

"*Ba.*"

Chemel herself went to tell Jiahano.

Chapter Eleven

Chemel should have enjoyed the occasion. She and Jiahano were actually allowed down in the valley. This was a time for work, not pleasure, true, and the ground lay hot and rocky beneath her bare feet while the sun's heat struck her like a hammer and the wind blew witheringly dry, sucking moisture from everything it touched. Still, they were out of the cave, with only Ala'ka watching them. Chemel's attention was not on her relative freedom, however. She dipped a small bowl into the jar of urine Ala'ka had flown down from the cave, poured the liquid bit by bit on the stretched, dried fly-goat hide before her, and as she worked it into the hide, she watched the sky above the mesa to the west.

The sky was empty. Not even a cloud or bird marred its brassy perfection. Chemel frowned. "Where are they? It's been ten days."

Jiahano worked on a bolki hide. "Patience, *mua.*"

"I hope the glider's working."

"Its capability was sufficiently demonstrated, I believe, before Ia'hi and She'shee's departure."

Chemel had played cargo on the test rides. What pleasure that had been, soaring high above the mesa behind Ia'hi and Ra'ab or Bi'nrar. The five-kord span of thin thunderfoot hide laced tight over the wooden frame had supported her weight easily at the time, but she could not feel confident about its construction or durability.

She moved closer to Jiahano so she could talk in a lower voice. "It's the first aircraft they've ever built. Look how long it takes other races to develop efficient aircraft."

"Most races, *mua*, do not have the advantage of already understanding aerodynamics, or having their own anatomy to serve as a model for wing design."

It still seemed that twelve days was too short a time to build their first glider. Something that came that easily must be faulty somewhere. She started to bite on a nail, then remembered what her hands were in and stopped short.

Ala'ka looked over the hide she was working and pointed to Chemel's hide. "You missed a place. The hide must be wetted all through."

Chemel added more urine to the spot. "I wish they'd let me go with them."

"The glider could not support your weight and that of the cargo as well."

She knew that. She was also aware she was fretting uselessly. That knowledge did nothing to stop the impatient pacing in her head. "Ia'hi came back in six days the first time."

"*Ga'aeree.*" Ala'ka's voice was sharp. "Work the hide."

Chemel worked it, but she watched the sky all the while. She finished the hide and laid it out on the ground to dry, then started another. She was halfway through that one when light flashed in the southern sky. She lifted her head.

"Sky signs. What do they say, Ala'ka?"

Ala'ka watched while the flasher's light looped across the sky. "The emres still be looking for *ga'aeree*. Thiil be coming to visit again soon."

Chemel swore. That Aranen again. "Perhaps we ought to do something about Thiil."

Ala'ka looked over at her. "What do you mean?"

Jiahano frowned. "Unwise. It would be witnessed and I do not propose to set such an example for our hosts."

Chemel stepped back mentally and looked at herself in horror. Just what was happening to her? She condemned the miners for intervention, but she was ready to show the Shree murder?

What would their reaction be to real violence? she wondered. Then she thought of G'han. Was it possible she might be able to solve that problem with the right approach?

Light flashed in the western sky. Chemel dropped the hide and jumped to her feet. The light flashed again. It did not move; there was no sky signing, just the light flaring again and again. She held her breath. They could hardly sky sign pulling the glider.

"Who is it? Can you tell?"

Ala'ka shook her lower shoulders. "They be a while coming. You can finish wetting the hide."

Chemel worked feverishly. Jiahano finished his hide and turned to help her. Together they had the hide worked through and spread out to dry beside the others by the time figures were distinguishable in the sky. Chemel cleaned her hands by rubbing them with the sandy soil and brushing them off on the thighs of her trousers.

"It be Ia'hi," Ala'ka said. She whistled piercingly.

Someone in the cave answered.

The broad-winged silhouette of the glider behind the two Shree made the identification simple. They were not alone, though. Above them flew a third figure.

Chemel rubbed a brow tuft. One of the mountain Shree coming along for a visit?

As they came nearer, the third flyer began to disturb her. The silhouette seemed wrong for a Shree. The wings looked different.

"Damn! It's an Aranen!"

What had happened? Had one of the mining supervisors met them somewhere and become suspicious enough to insist on tagging along? It might even be Thiil.

She looked quickly for a place to hide. What a time to be caught down in the valley. There was that plate-leaf tree where Ia'hi had waited for her to try escaping. Could she and Jiahano keep out of sight there? Could they reach it before the Aranen recognized that two of the figures in the valley were not Shree? "Head for the tree."

Jiahano did not move. "If we see them, they are surely able to see us."

"We can't just stand waiting for him to catch us." On the other hand, she thought an instant later, why not? He could not reach his communicator or any weapon while in flight and once he was on the ground, they were in a good position to overpower him. "All right, we'll stand. Get ready to jump him."

"Not to kill him."

"No," she agreed, "not to kill him." Though she would like to.

The cave entrances above them spilled whistling, clicking Shree into the air. They climbed in spirals and arabesques to meet the glider and to circle it in an impromptu wing dance. A dozen pairs of hands helped guide the glider toward the mesa top. Chemel lost sight of the Aranen in the swirl of winged forms. She started to panic. Perhaps the Aranen would land on the mesa, too, and call his superiors from there.

The wing dance proved too much of a temptation for Ala'ka. She leaped upward to join it.

Chemel pulled at Jiahano's sleeve. "Let's go. We can be well up the valley before they miss us."

"And the rest of the team?"

"Maybe we'd better worry about tripping the pick-me-up first, before we can be stopped permanently."

He moved after her.

Then from overhead came a shrill cry. They looked up to see the Aranen diving toward them. Chemel bent to pick up a large rock. She had stunned Thiil once before. She would do it again, if necessary, and this time she would not worry if she hit him too hard.

She never touched the rock. Instead, she straightened, staring, as the Aranen's features and aerie markings became recognizable.

"*Kiris!*" Chemel and Jiahano shouted in unison.

Kiris came out of the dive so close over their heads they instinctively ducked. She wheeled upward once more. Coming down, she slowed, and dropped to the ground in front of them. "Greetings."

The lisping accent was good to hear. Chemel touched one of Kiris's shoulders in disbelief. "Thiil said you were dead. He said he broke your wing and you fell."

Kiris blinked. "Thiil? That mishatched rotten-egg illegal?" She grimaced. "He just dislocated my shoulder. I went down, all right, but I still had one good wing, and even a dislocated wing can help slow a fall. Maybe I looked dead to him. When I hit the mountain I knocked myself out."

"Where have you been since then?" Jiahano asked.

"Some Shree found me. They thought I was an emre and when I found out what that was, I let them keep thinking it. I've been traveling around, visiting one band and another since." She paused, clicking her beak. "I . . . went back to the station the first thing after I could fly again. The hangar was open and there was no one there except—except some bones the scavenger birds had picked clean. Who was it?"

"Prol." Briefly, Chemel told her about it.

Kiris closed her eyes. "Oh, no."

"How did you happen to come back here with Ia'hi and She'shee?"

It was a minute or two before Kiris opened her eyes and answered. "I was visiting around, hoping to hear something about the rest of you. I didn't dare ask direct questions because up in the mountains the supervisors visit the Shree often enough they were bound to get word of someone asking for you. The band I was with saw the sky signing about trading skyeye for metal. They went to trade and I went, too. I remembered that there were two observation posts with pick-me-ups in the Firestone Territory, and I thought maybe if you were alive you would have headed for them."

Kiris traveled around. No one tried to keep her prisoner. Chemel sighed. Anyone with wings had a definite advantage with the Shree. "We've tried to reach them. You heard something about us at the trade?"

Kiris lifted her chin. Chemel noted it with amusement. So she had picked up the native gesture, too. "I've worked at learning the language and when your two band members saw me, I overheard the female— She'shee, I think?—mutter something to the male about being glad they hadn't let the *ga'aeree* come, that if they had, the emres would have found out about her. It seemed to me there could be only one group of aliens who would want to stay unknown to the miners, so I invited myself along on the return trip."

Chemel bit her lip. "And they just let you come?"

"They tried to talk me out of it by painting a terrible image of this area. I let them think I planned to fly just a day with them. Once we were away, though, I told them who I was. They pretended not to know what I was talking about. I described each of the team. When I reached you two they became so blank I knew they had to have seen you. So then I told them what your names are. I don't know if that was what decided them or not, but they let me come the rest of the way."

"We are truly glad to see you," Jiahano said.

"Truth." Chemel hugged her.

Kiris blinked in surprise at Chemel. "Do you know where the others are?"

"We're trying to find them." Chemel turned to look up at the rim of the mesa. Shree were carrying small loads down from the top to the cave. "That's what the metal is for."

One Shree not carrying anything was G'han. Instead, he flew around the edges of the activity.

Chemel whistled. Shree heads turned toward her. She called, "G'han."

His ears twitched.

"Come down. I want to talk to you."

He frowned but circled down in a slow spiral and dropped to his feet a short distance away, eyeing her suspiciously. "What do you want?"

She walked down the valley away from Jiahano and Kiris. "You've seen the sky signs that Thiil will be visiting us again?"

After a moment he lifted his chin.

"I hope you won't be tempted to sell us to him."

His upper lip pulled back from his teeth. "I may."

She kept moving, drawing him with her. "Do you know what the emres want with us?"

"I do not care."

She slid him a side glance. "They'll kill us when they have us."

G'han blinked. "Kill?"

Now was a good time to explain it. "Kill . . . cause *sa'ah,* death. *Ga'aeree* slaughter each other as the People kill meat animals."

G'han's eyes widened in horror, then he tucked in his chin. "They be only *ga'aeree.*"

"I feel considerably less indifferent, probably because it involves me personally." She glanced behind her. They had come a long way from the others.

"Maybe you'd care a bit more if it involved you personally."

He eyed her warily. "What do you mean?"

She swung to face him. "Being capable of killing our own kind, we're perfectly able to kill others, too. I, for example, might very well kill one of the People if I were angry enough."

G'han stepped backward. His wings started to spread, ready for full extension and flight. Chemel grabbed him by the wings, forcibly folding them and lifting him off his feet. His mouth opened but no sound emerged. His eyes filled his face. She shook him hard enough to whipsnap his head, then returned him to his feet.

"I may be only *ga'aeree,* but I'm bigger and stronger than you are, G'han. If you tell Thiil about us I'll take you apart joint by joint."

She turned and walked away, leaving him frozen on the spot where she set him. She looked back when she reached the skins spread out to dry on the ground and found him still standing there. She bent down to pick up the skins. All but the last were dry. When she straightened again, G'han was gone.

"What did you do?" Jiahano asked anxiously.

Chemel smiled at him in calm satisfaction and folded the skins over her arm. They felt as soft as the membrane of a young Shree's wings. "I offered him incentive to resist any temptation Thiil might offer. Shall we go see when Ia'hi intends to start looking for the others?"

She returned to the cave as she had come down, by Asegah's rope from the survival pack. When she reached the entrance, she waited for Jiahano to tie the rope around himself and, with a couple of Shree helping, she hauled him up.

Ia'hi paraded around his stack of metal. Some were merely flat pieces. Other pieces had already been formed into knife blades and spear points. There were even five cooking pots, which Ala'ka and Ibee fingered coveteously. Ia'hi shooed the females back.

"These be for trading."

"When will you start?" Chemel asked.

"Tomorrow. She'shee and I begin visiting D'aka'reen bands, looking for *ga'aeree*. When we know where they be, we will take metal to trade for them."

The next morning Chemel, wishing she could go along, watched Ia'hi and She'shee each fly off in different directions. How she hated being forced to just sit there doing nothing. Even with Jiahano and Kiris for company, the waiting was going to be difficult.

The waiting proved to be worse than difficult. Time passed with interminable slowness. Chemel envied Kiris's freedom. The Aranen woman was allowed to come and go as she wished, to work off any nervous energy flying. She was invited to join the hunts and wing dances. Chemel could fight off biting her nails and pacing the floor only by working at any chore she could find. She even did that when the rest of the band lay around doing nothing more than telling stories and sunning themselves.

The Shree regarded her industry with amazement. "*Ga'aeree* be strange. Why work when it be not necessary?"

Jiahano said, "*Mua*, be—"

She turned on him. "If you tell me just once more to be patient, I'll throw something at you . . . and I won't miss."

Ia'hi finally returned eight days later. Chemel was the first one to him when he touched rock. "Have you found them?"

"I have found two."

"Will their bands take a trade for them?"

Ia'hi's ears twitched. "Yes."

Chemel frowned. What did that ear twitch mean? She did not like the tentative note in his voice, either. "What's the matter? Do they want more than we have to give them?"

He shook his lower shoulders. "The matter be with the *ga'aeree*. They do not wish to be traded. They beg to stay with their bands."

Chemel stared at him in dismay. The team members *did not want to come?* That was a problem she had never considered. "Didn't you tell them the rest of us are here?"

"I cannot tell them. Shishi'ka—"

"Says we're to be held in secret." She sighed. "I know."

Chemel wanted to beat her head against the cave wall. Damn Shishi'ka. Damn these little savages, too. They were as stubborn as—as Virinians, she thought with sudden humor. So he would not tell the team where they were going, and as a result they did not want to go. Now what?

Her eyes fell on Kiris. *That* was what. "Take Kiris along. The bands can think she's an emre but my people will recognize her."

After Ia'hi and Kiris left, Chemel went back to counting days and looking for ways to fill time. She listened for the sound of wings in the sky outside. She also listened for the sound of a grid drive. If the sky signs were right, Thiil could be visiting any time. She watched for him, and she watched G'han.

The Shree kept his distance, eyeing her warily. He stayed away from the cave even on idle days and if she was sitting in the main entrance, he used another to enter or leave. During meals, he sat on the far side of the circle.

"Do you think fear was the proper approach to use with him?" Jiahano asked.

She sighed. "I don't know." He could be doing anything while he was out of the cave. He could be contacting Thiil. "I just don't know."

Thiil did not come. She'shee did, with the news that she had found the other three members of the study team. "They be close. If someone will come to hold the other tether, I can bring them back as we took you to the *mi'inae'mi* digging."

"I can go with you," Ch'ae offered.

She'shee looked around for another volunteer but all the hunters were suddenly busy gathering spears for a hunt. With a sigh, She'shee took Ch'ae with her.

Chemel returned to waiting.

This time, however, the waiting was brief. The next day Ia'hi and Kiris appeared with the glider—and a small passenger with golden eyes and graying hair. If Riga were surprised by the enthusiasm of Chemel's welcoming hug, she did not show it. She returned the greeting in kind.

"Are you finding everyone?"

"I think so. Are you all right?" Chemel asked.

Riga smiled. "Fine . . . though I hope I never have to eat another fish as long as I live. The Mi'inae'mi Lake band eats well but monotonously. I'm glad you found me when you did. The early fruits were starting to tempt me to see what kinds of wine I could make from them."

Chemel frowned. "You were going to make *wine* for the Shree?"

Riga flushed. "My family's been making wine for twelve generations. It's almost a genetic reflex." She smiled. "It would have made the fish bearable."

The Sun Cliff band liked Riga immediately. Chemel suspected it was as much for the fact she stood eye to eye with them as for her friendly personality. Chemel overheard Ibee asking, "Be other *ga'aeree* a normal size like you, or be most oversized like them?"

Riga grinned at Chemel, then replied solemnly, "Sad to say, the universe is mostly inhabited by giants."

Chemel was curious about the band that held Riga. "I didn't know there were any lakes in the Firestone Territory."

"It's on the northern edge."

"How did you get that far north? Were you traded?"

"Not exactly." Riga grimaced. "I escaped twice. I

was trying to reach the observation post. The last Shree to recapture me were from the lake band. I got farther north than I intended." She lowered her voice. "Are you planning an escape for us from here?"

"When everyone is together, yes."

Two days later She'shee brought Sheth in. He did not use his left arm, which had a noticeable deviation below the elbow where the bone was healing slightly crooked. Aside from that, he reported he felt well. Chemel thought he looked good. A glow of health shone out through the anthropologist's yellow skin and he seemed less angular than Chemel remembered him as being.

"The climate agrees with me," he said. "This has been almost like going home to the region on Cheolo where I was born."

The Shree were fascinated by him and started calling him Han'hir'a, big lizard.

Later the same day Ia'hi and Kiris brought in Akaara. The computer tech fell joyously on the rest of the team, hugging them so hard ribs creaked and threatened to break under the pressure. "People again! My sanity is saved."

"Was it that bad?" Chemel asked.

He rolled his eyes. "They have no concept of mathematics. Any number beyond the fingers of their hands is *many*, and therefore incomprehensible. My brain is atrophying. When are we getting out of here?" He asked the question in a voice that could be heard halfway across the Firestone Territory.

Chemel slapped a hand over his mouth. "We'll talk about it later."

A group of young Shree gathered around Akaara to stare at him. They compared the thickness of his wrists to theirs. The ratio looked about four Shree to one Asbrini.

His size impressed the adults less. "Many emres be like him."

Chemel supposed that mining companies would like

hiring their work crews from natives of heavy-gravity worlds like Asbrin. Despite tunnelers and other modern machinery, mining still required a lot of muscle.

She regarded the group with satisfaction. They were healthy, well able to travel hard and fast when the time came. Only Salah and Baezar remained missing, and She'shee should be bringing them soon. Chemel hoped it would be very soon. She was feeling more and more uneasy about that threatened visit from Thiil. She did not look forward to his arriving at the same time as one of the team did.

Three more days. Still no sign of Thiil, but She'shee had not returned with the last two members of the team, either.

Another day. The hunters and Kiris left to find meat. Chemel spent the day grinding grain and stretching a fly-goat hide and scraping it in preparation for curing . . . chores she could perform near the entrance where she could watch the sky. About mid-afternoon the hunters came back with three *n'n*, a kind of small wild pig, but there was still no sign of She'shee.

Kiris squatted in the entrance with Chemel. "We saw sky signs. Thiil is visiting a band about fifty thousand kord south and will be coming this way."

Chemel froze, heart jumping. "Today?"

"Ra'ab read the signs for me. He didn't tell me a day." Kiris paused. "Could he be suspicious? He's already been here once and found nothing, you said."

Chemel started scraping again. "He's one of your people. How would he think?"

Kiris considered. "In his place, I'd be terrified of being sentenced to ego-death, and if I didn't find dead bodies or alien bones near that wrecked sled, I guess I'd keep hunting until I disposed of the witnesses against me or was sure they had died of natural causes."

"Tell everyone to keep back, ready to duck into one of those tunnels if he comes."

Chemel scraped the hide, using even, rhythmic strokes, and with each one, cursing. She wished she had crushed Thiil's skull when he stuck his head out that observation window. She wished his wings would break or his scooter would crash.

She wished She'shee would come back with Salah and Baezar.

The sun had turned bronze and was sitting on the western horizon when a Shree whistle pierced the evening sky, followed by the thrum of wings. She'shee and Ch'ae appeared over the mesa from the east. Chemel hurriedly moved to give them landing room.

At first she did not recognize the passenger who rode in the harness beneath them. She wondered if there had been some mistake. Had they picked up a miner instead? That was a chilling thought, but she did not know where else they might have found another Virinian. Only as the woman unlaced the harness and pulled free of it did Chemel realize it was Salah. This Salah, though, was as lean and bony as Chemel, with skin patched pink and pale where she had burned and peeled repeatedly.

She smiled at Chemel. "I knew you'd find us."

Her confidence pleased Chemel. Chemel smiled back. "Are you all right? You look like they starved you."

"I'm fine. I've just been working hard." Salah turned up her hands. The palms were calloused and the nails broken off short. "I became one of the band gatherers."

Chemel raised her brow tufts. "They let you out of the cave? Weren't they afraid you'd try to escape?"

Salah looked back in surprise. "Why should I want to escape? You'd have had a much harder time finding me if I were moving around. I waited in one place for you."

Chemel was not sure if she approved of such a pragmatic attitude in this case. "What if I never came?

Would you have ever tried to reach the post and set off the signal?"

"Virinians are very dedicated. You couldn't fail." Salah paused. "I almost wish it had taken you longer to find me, though. I have some two thousand words of Shree vocabulary identified but I'm just sorting out the grammatical forms. The grammar is basically Pan, but it's been adapted to the three forms of Shree speech: sky speech, ground speech, and fight speech. I needed a little more time to work out the variations."

Chemel shook her head. How typical. She was a bit surprised to find it annoyed her less now than it would have in the past.

She looked past Salah to She'shee, who stood with wings extended, cooling off. "Was there trouble getting her? You were gone so long."

"There be no trouble."

Ch'ae said, "We went for her after we could not get the other one."

"Sh'sha," She'shee snapped at him.

"What does he mean, after you couldn't get the other one?" Chemel's voice was sharp, too.

She'shee bared her teeth at Ch'ae. "Your mouth be a daughter of the wind."

"What happened?" Chemel said.

"It be nothing, *ga'aeree.*"

Ia'hi appeared at Chemel's side. "I heard you say you cannot get the other one. What do you mean?"

For once Chemel was grateful for the silver Shee's sharp ears.

She'shee sighed. "The band will not trade for the other one. They wish to keep him."

"Won't trade?" Chemel's heart dropped. "What did you offer them?"

"Everything. They wanted nothing. What does it matter? We have so many other *ga'aeree.*"

Chemel bit her lip. The band holding Baezar must have a price, but if not metal, what then? And how was she going to push the Shree into looking for the other band's price? She'shee had a sound argument against putting further effort into the hunt. So now what did she do?

Chapter Twelve

It was a strange kind of conference, conducted over the evening and next morning with just one team member at a time, in single words or broken fragments of sentences. With the Shree attentive to every word and action of their "guests," though, a group meeting would not have had any chance of succeeding. The question up for discussion was the same one Chemel had asked herself: What did they do now? They could try to escape and reach the observation post, hoping Baezar could be located when the S and E ships arrived. Alternately, they could look for a way to collect Baezar, then go for the post. Chemel put both possibilities before them.

Akaara was the only one to produce an unqualified opinion. "Let's get out. I've had more than enough of living native. Look for Baezar later. If he's like the rest of us, he's considered a kind of performing pet and he isn't being mistreated, so there's no harm leaving him there a while longer."

Most of the team preferred waiting until they found

Baezar. Chemel wondered about their motives, but only Salah came out and said what Chemel suspected the others were thinking. "I don't mind waiting. I'll have a chance to work on my study of the language. Living right here with them is the best possible situation for that."

Chemel eyed her. "What if we aren't able to bring in Baezar? How long do you think we should wait then?"

Salah's answering smile was serene. "You'll find him."

But not too soon, please. Was that the rest of what Salah was thinking? With a sigh, Chemel moved over to Jiahano, hoping that he, at least, would offer wise counsel.

To her frustration, Jiahano refused to express an opinion at all. "I am biased. We all are. We are scientists, remember, and inclined to pursue our own interests regardless of greater consequences. You are the monitor, *mua*. You are the one among us dedicated to the DSC, who sees the issues in clear terms of right and wrong."

Chemel scowled unhappily. "Not lately."

Her frown deepened as she looked at him. What was wrong? They had been friends for a while, but now that the team was together again, he had retreated to his tower, from which he watched remote and untouched as before.

"Don't do this to me, Jiahano. I need help."

"Why? Surely you know what you want to do."

Of course she did, but . . . "What I want may not be right. I want to find Baezar before we escape, but is it because I feel responsible for him, or is it because sitting here and being passive is easier than taking action? If I stick strictly to DSC policy, I should take us out of here right now, but what long-term harm might come of leaving Baezar in their hands?"

"Long-term harm?"

"The Shree want aliens here. If they have Baezar, they'll hide him in order to keep him. S and E can't possibly make a fine enough search to find him. Baezar comes from a race as long-lived as yours and in this light gravity, he could live even longer than normal. He could be actively or passively affecting the Shree for a thousand years."

Jiahano's gaze was sympathetic. "Perhaps right and wrong is becoming more difficult to determine; however, you have an excellent mind. You do not need me to dictate answers to you."

His words echoed in her mind. Somewhere not long ago she had heard similar words. Something else tickled the back of her mind, too . . . something she had said. It eluded all her attempts to trap it, though, and when she went back over everything she had said to Jiahano, nothing evoked the response again.

However, she did think of an approach to convince the Shree that Baezar was worth finding something the Vulture Cliff band would accept in exchange for him. She went looking for Ia'hi.

She found him at an entrance, playing with Hib'aki's infant, and headed for him.

Before she could reach him, however, she was distracted by a bright flash. G'han stood in another entrance showing something shiny to Bi'nrar. Chemel halted, breath catching. What G'han held was a knife, gleaming new, with a black haft shaped for more fingers than a Shree hand had. She abruptly switched course toward him.

G'han saw her coming. Jamming the knife into a scabbard on his harness, he whirled for the entrance.

"G'han, you stay right there!" Around her, Chemel sensed Shree and team members turn to stare at her in surprise. She ignored them to concentrate on G'han.

She reached him just as his wings were spreading for flight. Grabbing the edge of the nearest wing, she leaned back and pivoted, swinging him with her. Halfway around, she let go, sending a screaming G'han rolling and sliding back into the cave.

Someone threw wiry arms around her from behind.

Without bothering to see who it was, Chemel reacted in defense, turning just enough to drive the edge of her hand into the other's groin and stamp the instep of one foot, then, as the grip on her loosened, she brought an elbow up hard into into the other's diaphragm. She heard an explosion of breath and was free.

She dived for G'han again. Catching the scruff of his neck, she hauled him to his feet and jerked the knife from the scabbard. The blade was stamped: *Kossa Steel, Eos.*

"Where did you get this? Did you get it from Thiil?"

G'han wailed in terror.

She shook him. "Screaming isn't going to earn you any comfort from me. Tell me where you got this blade!" She shook him harder. "Tell me *now!*"

G'han sobbed. "Thiil gave it to me."

Her grip tightened. "For what? Did you tell him about us?"

"No! I said nothing about *ga'aeree* here. I said nothing!"

"*Mua—*"

"Quiet, Jiahano. Then why did he give it to you, G'han? You must have earned it somehow. *How?*"

"I traded the folded picture for it."

Folded picture? What— She stared at him, aghast. "The map? You sold him the *map*?" She threw him down, swearing.

He landed flat on his stomach. He pulled in arms and legs but otherwise remained huddled, shrieking as if mortally wounded.

Chemel threw the knife down beside him, feeling sick. Thiil now had the map showing where the other observation post was.

"Kiris, do you—"

She stopped as she looked around and found herself surrounded by people whose faces were all eyes.

"Now I know how the Virinians once walked in and took over one world after another," Riga said.

"Yes." Sheth leaned against a rock column, holding his stomach.

Chemel forgot G'han and what she had been about to ask Kiris. "Did I hurt you? Are you all right?"

"Yes and yes, if my foot isn't broken and my diaphragm not ruptured. Fortunately my reproductive system is less vulnerable than a mammal's."

"I'm sorry. I didn't think. I saw G'han with the knife and—" She looked down at G'han, who howled again and crawled around behind Hir'a. "I'm sorry, G'han. I thought you'd sold us. You don't know it, but selling the map is almost as serious as selling us. Kiris, come with me, please."

She walked Kiris over to a far entrance, away from everyone. The Shree showed no interest in following her. They stepped well out of the way as she passed them.

"Did you ever see the map?" she asked Kiris.

"No, I'm afraid not."

"Then you don't know where the post is."

"No."

The fly-goat hide Chemel had stretched in a drying frame the day before leaned against the cave wall nearby. She brought it to the entrance. Using her fingernail as a stylus, she scratched a copy of the map on the hide, outlining mesas, valleys, and basalt towers while she explained how to find the entrance and work the lock combination. "Do you think you can find it from this?"

Kiris clicked her beak. "You ask an *Aranen* if she can find her way, wingless one? Yes, I'll find it."

"Just don't spend time looking at the scenery on the way. Thiil won't."

After Kiris departed, Chemel found Ia'hi. He eyed her warily. "Do not come too close, *ga'aeree*."

"I won't attack you," she said.

He did not appear very reassured.

"I want to know if you're still thinking of trading for the last *ga'aeree*," she said.

"The Vulture Cliff band will not trade."

"Baezar is our elder . . . very old and very wise. He was born in the time of your mother's mother's mother. You could learn a great deal from him."

"If he would teach us." Despite the dubious tone an acquisitive glitter jumped in his dark eyes. "So old? Like Shishi'ka?"

Something ticked at the back of her head again and fled before she could touch it. "No, he isn't quite immortal, but he's older than any of us. He's seen many worlds and many people."

Ia'hi rubbed an ear. "So that be why the band will not trade."

"There must be something they want enough to give him up."

She left him gazing into space with his forehead furrowed in thought and went to stand in the entrance to stare at the copper sky. How long would Kiris need to reach the post? It lay ninety thousand kord away. Two to three hours, perhaps? Kiris should be there and back by evening. Chemel hoped she arrived in time.

A whistle sounded in the sky. Chemel looked up. A copper-colored male she had never seen before dropped toward her.

She stepped back into the cave. "Stranger coming. Team, get into the tunnels."

They obeyed instantly. Salah, the last of them, vanished into the shadows at the rear of the cave just as the stranger touched rock. There was no time for Chemel to hide, though. Her mind raced, hunting for a story to explain her presence there.

She had a little time to think. The band swarmed toward the visitor to welcome him. Chemel noticed that She'shee hung back, though.

Ch'ae greeted the visitor by name, and introduced him to the rest of the band. "This be Hargah of the Vulture Cliff band."

Chemel stood straighter. Vulture Cliff band? Could he have come to discuss trading after all?

The conversation ran fast and in the confusing overlay of voices Chemel distinguished Hir'a's voice asking Hargah's business.

Hargah looked past them at Chemel. "You have a *ga'aeree,* too."

Chemel made herself approach him. "What's he saying? Speak Pan so I can understand. What band are you from?" Her conversation with the Mianai geologist outside the skyeye mine flashed through her mind. "I'm Athe Vren, hunter for the emres."

"She does not understand the People's tongue," Hir'a said in the Shree language.

"Good." Hargah proceeded to treat Chemel as if she were nonexistent. "I have come because I be curious why you wish to have a *ga'aeree.*" His eyes searched the group as he spoke, and brightened as they found She'shee. *"Ha t'k't."*

She'shee turned away without a reply. The other band members nudged each other and hissed through their noses in amusement. Chemel bit her lip. Another fool come chasing She'shee. Disappointment stabbed sharply. She had wanted the Shree to be interested in trading.

"Why don't you talk so I can understand you?" she complained. "I thought you were going to show me where to find a band of *t'kan'dan,* Ia'hi."

"Later, hunter," Ia'hi said in Pan.

Chemel sighed. "I'll wait, then." She squatted down in the entrance with her back against the stone.

Switching back to the Shree language, Ia'hi said, "The *ga'aeree* be an elder. You have had him, now we wish to learn from him, too."

Chemel watched the visitor's eyes follow She'shee as the female picked up a stretched piece of hide and her ink and stylus. Squatting in an entrance with a young Shree, she began drawing a picture of the *m'im* the young one held.

"We have metal to trade for the *ga'aeree,*" Ia'hi

said. "We have spear points, cooking pots, and pottery."

"The elders wish to keep the *ga'aeree*." Hargah walked away from Ia'hi to the entrance where She'shee squatted drawing. He flexed and resettled his wings, then squatted where he could see what she was doing. Chemel heard him begin telling She'shee about the superior hunting in the Vulture Cliff band's territory.

Ia'hi sighed. "They will not trade."

"I know what *he'd* trade Baezar for," Chemel said.

Ia'hi flattened his ears. "The People belong to themselves. They cannot be given or taken."

"Certainly not She'shee Ch'be."

Ia'hi blinked. "Ch'be?" He hissed through his nose. "You speak a truth. She'shee Ch'be. Hargah would be better trading *ga'aeree* than seeking her."

But of course none of the band would tell the visitor that. They were all content to let him court her while they watched gleefully. None took more malicious pleasure in it, either, than S's'lis and Ch'ae.

Chemel was puzzled, though. "He's talking about her going back with him. Isn't it the males who always change bands?"

"Not always."

Chemel wished she could find the courtship as entertaining as the band did. However, she kept wondering about Kiris, and at intervals she drifted back to the tunnels where the team hid.

"How long is he going to stay?" they asked after she told them who Hargah was and why he was there.

Chemel sighed. "I don't know. The last visitors who came courting She'shee haven't left yet."

That was no comfort at all to people sitting on cold stone in the dark.

She went back to the front of the cave, where Hargah was extolling his sexual prowess. She'shee did not look up from her meticulous drawing of the *m'im*. "*Z'z'ras* mate with great energy, too."

That stung him. He frowned. "I be a hunter of

z'z'ras. I have speared many of them out of the air. I sleep on *z'z'ras* pelts."

Chemel shuddered. Genetically, *z'z'ras* and *Ka'ch'ka* were identical. The only difference was the wild Shree had not been stimulated into using the intellectual capacity that lay dormant in their brains. To think of hunting them like fly goats was like hearing of mentally retarded Virinians being slaughtered for sport.

The wrinkle of She'shee's nose told Chemel the Shree female did not think highly of the idea, either.

Under other circumstances, Chemel might have admired Hargah's persistence. He absorbed all the punishment She'shee could hand out and still pursued her. On the other hand, perhaps he was just not very bright. Chemel sighed, wishing She'shee would end the game.

A whistle shrilled a landing warning outside. Chemel ran for the entrance. That was not a Shree whistle.

Kiris came down in a dive. As she landed, Chemel gestured toward Hargah. "For his benefit, we're Emre hunters. Did you find the post?"

Kiris sighed. "Yes."

The weariness in that single word said everything. Chemel's heart dropped. "But . . . not first?"

Kiris shook her head. "The pick-me-up was smashed beyond any hope of repair."

Chemel leaned her forehead against the cave wall and pounded the wall with a fist. She swore, softly but passionately.

"So, here we are almost all together and nowhere to go . . . no way to go home," Kiris said.

The words tolled in Chemel's head. No way home. Then she stopped pounding the wall and turned around. "There's still one more t-com on Ne'en."

"One more? Where—" Kiris's eyes widened and her beak fell open. "The *miners'*? But how can we possibly use that one?"

"I haven't the slightest idea, but if we're ever going

to reach DSC and clear everyone off this planet, we'll have to find a way."

"Perhaps I should let G'han trade you to the emres."

They spun, starting. Ia'hi glared at them, ears flattened against his head. "You sent Kiris to tell your worlds where you be," he said accusingly.

Chemel caught Kiris's eyes. Kiris grimaced. After a moment Chemel sighed; she might as well be truthful. "I sent her, but the machine she needed won't work. We can't reach our people now."

"You wanted all your people. You tricked me into gathering them."

From her height, avoiding his eyes was easy, but she made herself meet his gaze. "Yes, I did."

"Why?" His forehead wrinkled. The question had almost as much curiosity and puzzlement in it as anger. "Why do you wish to leave? We feed and care for you. We want you."

She leaned her head back against the stone and closed her eyes. Every time she tried to tell them, she always failed to make them understand. How could she possibly do better this time? Still . . . why not try?

She opened her eyes again. "My people have rules. Rules," she explained as she saw his forehead wrinkle questioningly, "are statements telling us what we must or must not do. Our rules say Ne'en belongs to the People and that only the People may live on Ne'en. Everyone else, emres and *ga'aeree*, must leave."

"Your rules!" His wings opened and closed with a snap. His voice cut like a fine surgical blade. "If you speak truth, then how can you bring *your* rules to *our* world?"

The words reverberated like a gong inside her. She had DSC-policy answers to his questions, of course. The rules were for the People's benefit. The DSC and Sodality knew best, being an old civilization that had made many mistakes and now realized each race should progress in its own way. She had said all this one way or another before, though, and just now the points seemed feeble. DSC *was* imposing its own rules on this world . . . and how did they *know* it was best for Ne'en? Chemel did not know, not any longer. Right and wrong. she thought with a sigh, were not only becoming difficult to determine, they were becoming impossible.

"I'm going to have to think about this. Meanwhile, can we get rid of Hargah so my people don't have to sit in the dark and go hungry?" She paused. "And I'd still like to bring Baezar in, if we can."

He eyed her with suspicion. "You will try to leave when all of you be together."

She thought and decided quickly. "Not now. Until I find a way to reconcile my rules and your world, I won't do anything without discussing it with you first. That is a truth."

He considered, then looked around at She'shee and Hargah on the far side of the cave. He whistled. "She'shee, come."

She did as she was told with what looked very much like relief. Hargah tried to follow, but stopped when she snarled at him. She came on alone, forehead furrowed.

"Has he talked about the *ga'aeree*? Does he say what he might take in trade for him?" Ia'hi asked her.

She'shee snorted. "He talks only of himself."

"Will you ask him what he will trade?"

"I do not wish to ask him anything. I wish to be rid of him. His mouth is a daughter of the wind. Nothing I say to him drives him away. He says he will stay until I—" She broke off, a thoughtful look coming into her eyes. "You wish him to trade for the *ga'aeree*?"

Ia'hi lifted his chin.

She bared her teeth. "I will help. Hargah!"

The visitor perked up instantly. While he was on his way, She'shee lowered her lip back over her teeth. "You wish me to go back to your band with you and be your mate?"

Hargah panted in his eagerness. "*Ba!*"

She'shee regarded him haughtily. "I will come."

He started to dance.

"If you will take blades and pots in trade for the *ga'aeree*."

His dance stopped. His ears twitched. "I cannot speak for the band."

She'shee sniffed. "You say you be the leader."

He was less than definite. "*Ba.*"

"When you trade the *ga'aeree*, then I will come to be your mate."

Chemel was startled, and moved. She would never have considered She'shee capable of this kind altruism. Where did it come from, loyalty to the band, or was it loyalty to Ia'hi personally?

Hargah frowned, biting at his fingernails.

She'shee bared her teeth. "You cannot do it?"

He lifted his chin. "I can do it. I will go to do it now." He walked to the entrance and leaped out.

They stared after him.

"You're sure you want to do this?" Chemel asked her.

She'shee's eyes glittered. "I wish it."

Chemel reflected that if she were Hargah, she would not like the expression she saw in She'shee's eyes just now. Hargah was going to pay dearly for his passion.

Then she forgot about him as she went back to tell the team they could come out now.

Chapter Thirteen

"It's a trade!" Kiris snapped her beak in excitement. "The sky signs passed on from the Vulture Cliff band say Baezar is on his way. He'll be here soon."

Chemel felt satisfaction but no real excitement. She slipped away from the others and went to sit on her sleeping hide. After they were all together, then what? Eight extra mouths, seven of them belonging to people essentially useless for hunting or gathering, were going to place a considerable burden on the band. How long would they tolerate it?

That argued for leaving, but then came the question of where they could go. She had still not thought of a way to reach the miners' t-com. Even if she did, she would have to tell Ia'hi and obtain his permission to go. There was also the matter of DSC regulations versus Shree wishes. If the team found a way to leave and the Shree did not want them to go, should they then stay? Trying to resolve the conflict gave her a headache.

She believed in answers. Her father had always

preached that all problems had solutions, that finding the solution was simply a matter of assembling the facts and applying them to a logical formula. It had not seemed to work here. Maybe she had not come up with the right logical formula yet.

Chemel became aware of movement beside her. She looked up into She'shee's eyes.

"I be leaving," She'shee said.

The price of the trade! Chemel stood up. "I'll miss you." She paused. "You don't like Hargah. Why are you doing it?"

She'shee's upper lip pulled back from her teeth. "To shame him."

Chemel blinked, then sighed. So much for altruism. "How does this accomplish that?"

"I will take his *ga'aeree* and give him only blades and pots in trade. He will not have what he wants."

"But . . ." Chemel frowned. "You said you'd go with him."

The bared teeth looked more like a grin than a snarl. "I did not say I would *stay*."

Chemel knew she should disapprove of the Shree female's shameless deceit, but she found herself fighting back a chuckle.

"I have helped find all your people," She'shee went on. "Perhaps when I return you will answer some of my questions?"

This time Chemel could not help laughing. She might have known that request would follow. "Perhaps."

At the front of the cave someone cried out. "They be coming!"

She'shee looked toward the voice, then reached out to draw a finger down Chemel's arm. "*Ha t'k't.*"

Chemel looked back a moment in silence. Her throat felt suddenly tight. "*Ha t'k't,*" she replied.

She'shee swung away. Walking to a small entrance, she leaped out.

At the main entrance, the team moved quickly back

toward the rear of the cave, out of sight. The band stood aside to give the newcomers landing room. Chemel decided she could play hunter again and moved up to join the band.

One of the flyers was Hargah, no doubt coming along to escort his new mate back to his band. The other was probably another member of the band. Between them, Baezar hung in a harness modified to a sling. He landed quickly after Hargah, running.

The band looked him over curiously, but less so than they had some other members of the team. Chemel decided he must not be a curiosity to them. After all, as a hexapod, he was not that different from local life forms. She did hear one sharp gasp, however, and turned to see Hir'a staring wide-eyed at Baezar. His lips moved, but Chemel heard no sound from them.

Chemel lifted a brow tuft. She studied Hir'a, then Baezar. She wished she were able to read Hir'a's lips. Why did the sight of Baezar startle the aging hunter?

"We will spend the night with you and return to our band tomorrow," Hargah said.

While the team went hungry and slept on the stone of the tunnels? Chemel swore.

From the sky outside came She'shee's voice, "*I* be leaving *now*." Wings thrummed.

Hargah yelped and whirled to leap out the entrance. Snarling, his fellow band member followed.

The team must have been watching. With the visitor gone, they raced up to fling themselves on Baezar, hugging him and ruffling his mane—all talking at once.

Chemel contented herself with waving at him from where she stood. She ran a hand through her hair. What did Hir'a see when he looked at Baezar? Why did he see it when no one else did?

At her side, Ia'hi said, "It be still a truth that you will not escape now that you have all your people?"

"It's still truth."

"It be a truth that he be most elder of all the *ga'aeree*?"